'I think I'd be completely wrong for the job.'

'I should think you would want, I don't know. . .someone glamorous, with the right looks,' Sally began.

'On the contrary. I want a person who's warm and friendly, to give a more homely image,' Neil said.

'Thanks a bunch. I've been called a few things in my time, but never homely before,' Sally snorted. 'That's an American way of saying plain, isn't it?'

Dear Reader

March winds blow us good reading this month! Christine Adams' SMOOTH OPERATOR shows the useful as well as glamorous side of plastic surgery, while Drusilla Douglas has two sisters apparently after the same man in RIVALS FOR A SURGEON. Abigail Gordon's A DAUNTING DIVERSION is a touching story of a twin left alone to find a new path in life, and we welcome back Margaret Holt with AN INDISPENSABLE WOMAN. Enjoy!

The Editor

Christine Adams is a registered nurse, living in the West Country, who has worked for many years in the National Health Service and still nurses part-time. She has been writing for the past ten years, mainly short stories and articles. She finds the drama and tensions in the medical world an ideal background in which to find plots and storylines.

Recent titles by the same author:

TROUBLED HEARTS
LOVE BLOOMS
DEMPSEY'S DILEMMA

SMOOTH OPERATOR

BY
CHRISTINE ADAMS

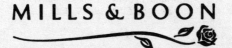

MILLS & BOON LIMITED
ETON HOUSE, 18-24 PARADISE ROAD
RICHMOND, SURREY TW9 1SR

MILLS & BOON, the Rose Device and LOVE ON CALL are trademarks of the publisher.

*First published in Great Britain 1995
by Mills & Boon Limited*

© Christine Adams 1995

Australian copyright 1995

ISBN 0 263 14295 7

*Set in Times 10 on 12 pt. by
Rowland Phototypesetting Limited
Bury St Edmunds, Suffolk*

15-9501-44485

Made and printed in Great Britain

CHAPTER ONE

'Is THE collar very uncomfortable?' Mrs Shelby asked sympathetically.

'Not too bad,' Sally murmured, keeping her head and neck carefully in line as she looked towards her friend at the top table, managing to smile in spite of the harshness of the surgical collar against her skin.

Even with the evidence of her own eyes it was difficult to believe that Jane Shelby and Matthew Carvalho had finally made it to the altar, but there they were in all their glory. And Sally, who normally never cried at weddings, had a job to hold back the tears at the sight of the happiness on Jane's face, radiant beneath the cloud of ivory lace.

Though perhaps it wasn't sentiment that had brought the lump to Sally's throat; perhaps she was just feeling sorry for herself, for the happiness of the newlyweds contrasted so sharply with her own sorry state that it was difficult to bear, thrilled though she was for the new Mrs Carvalho.

She glanced round the room, her thoughts straying for a moment from the day.

It was a pity that Tom couldn't have been with her. But then he wasn't one to enjoy the traditional things in life, and would probably not have accepted the invitation even if he'd been at hand, instead of three thousand miles away in the sunshine of Texas. He must have thought her a fool. She'd been so sure he'd ask her to go with him and had even resigned from her job as staff nurse. She cringed in her seat, remembering his embarrassed astonishment, his casual farewell. 'Of course I'll write,' had been his final words, but she had known they were merely a sop to his conscience, a desire to avoid any tearful scenes.

With a tightening of her generous mouth, her hazel eyes shadowed in anger, Sally pushed aside the feelings of rejection and concentrated once more on the assembled guests.

It was a comparatively small gathering, but the goodwill towards the happy couple was almost palpable, the laughter and conversation rising in volume as the meal progressed and, with it, the steady consumption of wine.

Though he doesn't seem too full of goodwill, thought Sally, her eyes drawn to the man on the far side of the T-shaped arrangement of tables. The stiffness of her injured neck made it difficult for her to look directly at him but she was conscious, even from across the room, of cool grey eyes, partly screened by thick lashes, and dark hair brushed back from a sun-tanned forehead that was creased in a travesty of a frown.

As if aware of her gaze, the man stared back, and a small flicker of mischief made Sally raise her glass of wine in a salute; she was surprised at how it pleased her to be rewarded by the suggestion of a smile from his wide, sensual mouth.

Who on earth is he? she frowned to herself, curiosity lifting her spirits. But she hadn't time to wonder any further, for the speeches had begun, and once more

Sally's thoughts were drawn to her friends and the happiness on both faces.

'Sally! Here a minute!' Jane's voice reached her above the noisy chatter as the speeches drew to a close and, standing carefully, Sally moved through the now milling groups of people to reach the impatiently beckoning figure of the bride.

'Thank goodness you could come.' Jane reached towards her with an eager hand and pulled Sally into the adjacent seat. The new Mrs Carvalho's expression stiffened momentarily, the radiant light on her face darkening as though a cloud had drifted across the sun. She stared intently. 'Are you all right? I think Tom should be. . .' she hissed, not waiting for Sally to answer, her sense of outrage obvious.

Sally smoothed the turquoise material of her skirt down over her long legs, breathing in the scent that drifted from the bouquet of freesias and stephanotis on the table, and grinned back at Jane's aggrieved look.

'Forget about my love-life, you idiot. This is your day, and everything is meant to be all lightness and enjoyment.'

'It is.' Jane's eyes softened as she gazed towards her dark-haired groom, whose bulk shielded his companion from Sally's view.

'You look pretty well, all things considered,' Jane continued. 'Is the neck giving you much trouble now?'

Sally patted her friend's hand. 'I'm fine and it's only another couple of weeks before I get rid of this wretched collar. Anyway, enough of that. This is your day and you should be savouring every moment, not worrying about my stupid problems.'

Jane flung back her head and laughed. 'All right. I'll do as you suggest.'

'There is one thing, then I'll leave you in peace.' Sally leant forward and muttered confidentially, 'Tell me, who is the stern-looking man in the charcoal-grey suit, the one with cold grey eyes? He was sitting. . . .' Sally moved awkwardly on her chair. 'He was sitting just over there, and looked far from happy. . . Oh.' She paused uncertainly.

'I'll introduce you.' Jane smiled mischievously and pointed towards the tall figure next to her brand-new husband.

'Oh,' Sally muttered again, at a loss for words as she wondered if the man had heard her comments.

'Neil, come and meet my best friend. Sally, Neil Lawrence, an old friend of Matthew's. He's a surgeon. Neil, this is Sally Chalmers, and please be nice to her, for she's had a rough time lately.'

'How do you do?' The words were hurriedly spoken as he shook Sally's hand before turning away to move down the length of the room.

'Hmm, what's up with him?' Jane grimaced.

'Probably scared that you were about to tell him all my troubles,' Sally muttered, strangely hurt at the unexpected rebuff. She certainly wasn't having much success with men lately, what with Tom, and now Matthew's friend.

'He wasn't to know that I'd never push myself where I'm not welcome,' Sally muttered, trying to be fair. 'Anyway, enough of me——' she smiled at her friend '—it must be nearly time for you to leave.'

Jane nodded and gave a shiver of happiness as Sally went back to her seat, perching awkwardly on the edge of a chair.

Typical hospital gathering, she thought, even if it is a wedding. She tuned in to the various conversations that came her way as the reception gradually reached its end. 'I tell you, I thought we'd lost him. I've never seen such a rapid reaction to halothane. . .' 'Have you heard the results of the new patient-controlled analgesia trial? I reckon they should stick to morphine. . .' 'Can you possibly cover my night-shift on Tuesday. . .?'

Impatient that none of it involved her, Sally turned to Jane's mother. 'She looks lovely, doesn't she?' Sally murmured, ignoring the suspicious brightness in Muriel Shelby's eyes.

'She certainly does. I sometimes wondered if they'd actually make it.' Mrs Shelby smiled through her tears. 'But you never know how things will turn out.' Jane and Matthew had reappeared—Jane looking more her usual self in tailored trousers and a cream-coloured blouse.

Amid the chorus of farewell shouts and catcalls and the clicks of the cameras Sally stood back, lonely and, unusually for her, unsure, as the crowd waved to the departing car.

'Everything's so flat after a wedding,' she murmured to herself, drifting aimlessly round the room as the guests gradually disappeared, unable to decide what to do but sure that the last thing she wanted was to spend the evening on her own. The thought of her empty apartment, most of her belongings packed in anticipation of a move with Tom, was so unappealing that anything would be an improvement.

She rested a moment on one of the gilt chairs, ignoring the caterers as they cleared the dishes around her, and slowly untwisted her soft turquoise scarf, smoothing at where the ugly surgical collar had rubbed a sore place on the sensitive skin under her ear.

She heard no footsteps approach on the thick carpet and couldn't prevent a small cry of pain as the abruptly spoken words behind her made her jump and wrench her neck.

'Still here, then?' She recognised the voice immediately. Neil Lawrence moved round from behind her and stared at her curiously. 'Sorry, didn't mean to startle you. Are you waiting for someone? I thought all the guests would have gone by now. I came back because I've mislaid a cufflink.'

He flashed an edge of snowy-white shirt-cuff towards her, and she stared at the long, yet powerful fingers. Typical surgeon's hands, she thought, surprised at a sudden wish to touch those hands, knowing instinctively that they'd give comfort.

'The cufflinks are of great sentimental value,' Neil continued, his eyes glancing over the floor as he spoke. 'I'd hate to lose one, so I thought I'd come back now that everyone, well——' he smiled '—nearly everyone has gone.'

He paused, waiting for her to speak. But Sally couldn't think of a thing to say. She straightened, suddenly realising that she'd barely heard his words, for she'd been immersed in the texture of his voice, one of the most attractive she'd ever listened to—dark and smooth like chocolate, it seemed to envelop her in an unexpected sensation of warmth.

'Sorry.' She smiled an apology. 'Er. . .where do you think you might have dropped it?' Perhaps she was misjudging him, but she couldn't imagine his having a sentimental attachment to anything. 'Was it a present?' She leant forward, carefully supporting her chin in her hand.

'Yes, a present from someone very dear.' His voice was muffled as he moved away, peering at the ground all the while.

Probably some dazzling well-groomed female, thought Sally, pushing her hair back from her face, its dark flyaway texture suddenly irritating.

'Perhaps one of the caterers has found it. Would you like me to ask. . .?'

'Aha.' The small cry of triumph drew her attention back to her companion as he straightened and held aloft an object that sparkled, even in the dim light of the room.

'Damn, I can't get it to sit straight. Would you mind?'

He moved swiftly round two tables, the bare wooden surfaces stark now that their fine drapery had been cleared away, and took her hand, pressing the cufflink into her palm.

She couldn't for the life of her understand why her hands should tremble as she carefully pushed the link through the small holes of his shirt-cuff. All the while she was acutely aware of expensive cologne, of well-shaped nails cut short, of the soft sound of his breath as he concentrated on what she was doing.

Sitting back with a sigh of relief as she finished, Sally glanced up.

'Thanks. That's great. Well, I'll be off. See you around.' He walked swiftly through the double doors that led into the street.

'Come on, Sally, my girl, get yourself moving.' It's funny how lonely you feel on your own, after being one of a pair, she thought, yearning for even Tom's offhand company. She strolled outside, trying not to shiver as the early evening sun hid behind a patch of cloud and the spring breeze, rattling the branches of a nearby oak, cut through the filmy material of her dress.

There was no sign of Neil's tall figure in the street, only the caterers' van where they packed the last of their trays and crates, laughing and talking among themselves. Sally stood aside to let the last of them pass.

'Hey, want a lift, or are you waiting for someone?'

The shout was totally unexpected and for a minute Sally couldn't believe that Neil was talking to her. But a vigorously beckoning arm gestured from the window of a red hatchback, its engine revving noisily and belching out fumes.

'If it's not too much trouble, I'd love one.' Quickly Sally hurried to the far side of the car, and looked in. 'But won't it take you out of your way?'

Neil shrugged. He'd removed his jacket and the crisp whiteness of his shirt emphasised his broad shoulders. 'I don't know until you tell me where you're headed.'

'Just back to my lonely room.' She had meant her words to sound joking, but cringed at her downbeat tone. 'Sorry, I didn't mean to sound so pathetic. I live not far from St Adhelm's Hospital; it's handy for work.' Sliding awkwardly into the passenger side and clicking the seatbelt in place, Sally stared ahead through the windscreen. 'If you're sure it's not too much trouble.'

'You work at the hospital, do you?' He put the car into gear and edged neatly away from the kerb.

'I did, until my notice last month.'

'So what's next?'

'I'm not at all sure. I had plans but they didn't materialise. And now everything's been upset by my neck injury. I can't think about another job in general nursing at the moment, because I can't do any lifting. What about you? Where do you work?'

Abruptly she deflected the conversation from herself. She didn't feel like talking about her problems, and anyway she was very curious about the tall, good-looking man beside her. She'd worked in and around the local hospitals for the past four years, ever since she'd qualified, and she'd never come across this man before. Nor heard his name.

She glanced at him shyly. 'Jane said you're a surgeon, didn't she? What speciality?'

'I have my own clinic. It's not far from the esplanade, in one of those big Victorian houses at the opposite end from the shopping precinct.'

Own clinic, eh? 'So you're not in general surgery?'

'No. I recently moved here from London. Thought the bracing air of the Gloucester countryside might help my patients.' He glanced in the rearview mirror, moved out into the middle of the road, and skimmed past a tanker lorry that, fully laden, crept ahead of them along the narrow highway.

'Phew, that was a bit close,' Sally gasped nervously.

'You're not a back-seat driver, are you? I could see quite clearly,' he said sternly, then grinned, taking the sting from his words.

'Nothing used to worry me, but I'm a bit more wary since a car skidded into mine and I got this whiplash injury.'

'Sorry, I didn't realise that that was how you had hurt your neck. I'll take it more steadily from now on. Now, how about some directions, for we're nearly at the main hospital entrance.'

Sally stared from the car window as they approached the hospital, surprised that they'd arrived so quickly. She'd been too busy wondering about her companion to notice their whereabouts.

'If you drop me at the main gates, I can walk from there.'

'Don't be silly. I'll take you home.'

'All right, thank you. It would be nice, especially as the weather looks so threatening and I'm not really dressed for storms.' She couldn't control another shiver as she glanced at the greying sky with distaste, then down at the thin, silky turquoise material of her dress. 'Do you know Barton Road, that runs up behind the cathedral?'

He nodded. 'I was brought up near here. I know it very well.'

'My flat is the top floor of one of the three-storey houses at the end.'

'Right.' He plunged once more into the traffic and in moments they were at Sally's address.

'Would you like a coffee?' She was reluctant for him to leave, dreading the moment when she'd be alone.

He glanced at a paper-fine gold watch on his wrist. 'I'm afraid I can't stop now, but if you're free later how about we go for a meal? I gather that you're rather at a loose end, and I'd be glad of some company. Time after a wedding is always an anti-climax, isn't it?'

Moving awkwardly Sally turned, and looked across the car. 'You don't have to feel sorry for me, just because my dopey friend said. . .'

'Hush.' He rested a finger lightly on her protesting mouth. 'I don't spend time with people because I feel sorry for them. I'm on my own tonight; possibly I'm even lonelier than yourself, and I'd be glad of company, I promise you.

'Well, in that case, thank you very much,' Sally muttered breathlessly, leaning back into the car seat as he stretched across and opened the door.

'What shall I wear?'

'After this formality, I reckon something casual wouldn't go amiss. Do you like Italian food?'

'Love it, but I'm the messiest person in the world with a fork full of spaghetti.' She laughed, a lightening of spirits sweeping through her at the thought of the evening ahead.

'Right, you can have something more manageable. See you at about eight?'

'I'll look forward to it.' She waved, waiting at the edge of the pavement, a puzzled frown creasing her forehead as the small car moved away. If she'd been asked to guess what sort of car Neil had, she'd have picked something much more expensive than the rather battered hatchback that was fast disappearing from view. It gave a very different picture from her original assessment. But then at first acquaintance she'd misjudged him completely, thinking him surly and rather rude. And in contrast, during the drive, he'd been charm itself.

Taking her key from her bag, Sally hurried inside and plodded up the stairs.

You should never decide about someone straight away, she told herself sternly, opening the door of her flat and kicking off her shoes with a sigh as she went inside.

God, what a mess! She gazed round the sitting-room and grimaced with relief that Neil hadn't taken up her invitation for coffee. Absorbed in his company, she'd forgotten the state of the flat, the stack of books that spilled from the corner table, the duvet covers in a large plastic carrier, the scattering of letters that she'd started to sort which lay across the settee in a paper snowstorm.

'Blast you, Tom. I hope Texas is so hot it fries your brains.'

Unable to stifle a giggle as she caught sight of her scowling face in the mirror on the far wall, Sally gathered an armful of books and papers and hurried to the bedroom that stretched across the rear of the Edwardian house; even the double bed and old-fashioned wardrobe that her mother had given her were dwarfed by the tall sash windows and high ceiling.

Opening the bottom drawer of her whitewood chest, she pushed the bundles in willy-nilly and hurried back to the sitting-room, hiding papers under cushions, settling the rest of her books into an even pile, hurling the carrier into the sideboard. She didn't know if Neil was likely to come in for coffee later, but if he did she wouldn't want to give him the impression that she was a complete and utter slut!

'That's better.' She glanced at her handiwork, then went to the tiny kitchenette that was little more than a cubicle and filled the kettle, getting a mug from the overhead cupboard, spooning in instant coffee and adding the water after it boiled.

Absently she fished the remains of some chocolate biscuits from an open packet and carried them, with the mug of steaming black coffee, back to the living-room, flung herself awkwardly on to the edge of the settee and stretched her long legs out in front of her.

Why on earth she'd burnt her boats so dramatically when she'd heard about Tom's new post, she couldn't imagine. Her clear hazel eyes darkened in remembered pain as she thought again of the horror on Tom's face when she'd said she'd handed in her notice at the hospital, the unpleasant goodbye scene and his hurried departure.

Well, that was all water under the bridge, and she would have to decide exactly what she was going to do in the future. One thing she was sure of: she'd never accept anything any man said at face value again. Once bitten, a hundred times shy!

'Forget all that,' she told herself firmly. 'You have a dinner date that you didn't expect. Just be grateful for that and forget Tom.' The thought of it brought a flutter of nervousness. Or perhaps it was merely an anticipatory pang of hunger that stirred her stomach.

Very romantic, she grinned to herself. And as for Neil, why on earth was such an attractive man unattached, on his own after the wedding and looking for a dinner date? She hoped it wasn't that he felt sorry for her; she'd never forgive Jane for blabbing if that turned out to be the case.

'Don't put yourself down,' she told the mirror. 'However Tom may have behaved, you're still attractive enough to warrant an invitation in your own right.' She pouted dramatically and half closed her eyes. 'I look as though I'm about to be sick,' she giggled. 'Must remember not to try that expression on Neil or he'll be rushing me to Casualty for a quick stomach-pump.'

Whatever the reason he'd asked her out she was sure she would enjoy his company, and she had no intention of looking a gift-horse in the mouth.

Draining the last of her coffee, Sally went to her bedroom once more and began riffling through the contents of the wardrobe.

Wonder what Neil calls casual, she thought, picking out jeans, then discarding them. She could just picture him with a selection of cool sophisticates, well-groomed and expensively dressed. Somehow the heavy denim didn't seem appropriate. After a lot of thought she settled on black velvet trousers and a white silky blouse, both garments simply cut and relying on the richness of the material for effect.

She was ready far too early, her make-up understated, her hair held back by a clip, the bones of her face more clearly defined by the severe hairstyle, and for once she was not worried that the surgical collar was visible.

She switched on the television, flicked through the pages of a magazine, then eventually sat quietly on the settee and waited for Neil to arrive. And she was taken aback at the way her heart raced when the buzzer from the front door finally sounded in the flat.

'You look great.' He smiled in approval as Sally opened the main front door and glanced up at him, breathing in a drift of sharp-scented aftershave. 'I booked a table, so there's no rush. Would you like to go for a drink somewhere first? Or we could go straight to the restaurant if you're hungry.'

'Straight to the restaurant, please.' Sally was suddenly shy as he took her elbow in a strangely old-fashioned gesture and ushered her towards the car, the soft material of his maroon cashmere sweater making her shiver as it brushed against her.

'Not cold, are you? Well, the heater takes a bit of time to work, but I think you'll be warm enough in the car.' He shut the door gently behind her and went to the far side, his movements economical yet with a masculine grace.

Hmm, she thought, definitely a puzzle that he should be on his own. But I'm not complaining, certainly not. And she shifted herself more comfortably into the seat as Neil switched on the engine of the car and moved away from the kerb.

'What exactly do you do at your clinic?' Sally pushed the last spoonful of cassata ice-cream round her plate. The spaghetti carbonara had been delicious and she'd managed to eat it without disaster; she'd savoured the dryness of the wine but what she'd most enjoyed had been the easy conversation which had flowed between Neil and herself.

He was an attentive host, surprisingly witty, and they'd discovered some mutual acquaintances in the medical field, one or two of whom he'd imitated with a deadly accuracy, his grey eyes alight with mischief, the dark brown voice that had the power to prickle her spine changing its timbre, so that she laughed loudly enough to attract the glances of other diners in the restaurant.

Now the end of the evening was approaching far too quickly, and she still knew very little about her escort. She was surprised at how curious she was about him, at how much more she wanted to know.

'So, what do you do?' she repeated.

'I specialise in cosmetic surgery.'

'What, face-lifts, boob-lifts, chin-lifts?' Her voice rose incredulously. 'I wouldn't have pictured you in that field in a million years.'

'Why not?' He spoke quietly, suddenly defensive. 'Is there something wrong with helping people who want to improve their looks?'

'No,' Sally murmured doubtfully. 'I don't think I've really thought about it, but. . .' She laughed nervously.

'But if you had, you'd think of it as being trivial, not to be counted as a true branch of medicine?' He forced a smile, but his underlying expression was wary. 'Well, that's my chosen line of work, and I enjoy it. What about you? What made you choose nursing as a career, for example, where does your family live, are you from around here?'

'My life isn't very interesting. A farmer's daughter

who likes people better than animals,' she laughed. 'What made you pick on this area?'

'It was my grandmother's doing. She died last year, and as well as her house she left enough money for me to set up my own clinic in the way that I want.'

'And are your parents local?'

'Originally, yes. Both doctors. They took early retirement—unusual for doctors, isn't it?—and are spending a couple of years travelling to all the places they didn't have time to see when they were working.'

'Oh.' Sally paused, unable to think of anything else to say. There was no way she could ask the question at the forefront of her mind. Is there a Mrs Lawrence? He didn't have the look of a married man, if there was such a look. Was he one to play the field, perhaps? 'I hope I haven't offended you, when I said that about cosmetic surgery,' she began in a low voice. 'I can't pretend to know much about it, but I must confess it's never seemed like 'proper medicine' to me.' Nervously she crumbled the remains of a bread-roll between her fingers. 'Do you work with ordinary plastic cases, like burns and so on?' Desperately she wanted to believe that he was in medicine because he cared, not just for financial gain! And she didn't stop to analyse why it was so important to her.

'It's a pity you feel as you do,' he murmured, apparently reading her thoughts. 'I was going to ask you if you'd be interested in some temporary work at the clinic.' He leaned back from the table as the waiter came and set a tray in front of them, and was silent while the man poured the coffees then left. 'Oh, would you like a liqueur?'

Sally shook her head, too dumbfounded at his unexpected offer to speak.

'What's the matter? Is it that much of a shock, my asking you if you'd like a job?'

'Well, yes. I don't know anything about cosmetic surgery, or plastics in general, come to that. I've never worked in Theatre, except for a few weeks during my training.' She sipped her coffee, savouring its aroma, using the moment to try to gather herself together.

'I don't want someone for Theatres; I've an excellent Theatre sister. I want someone to act as nurse-receptionist—greet the clients when they arrive, explain procedures to them, generally be around as a support if and when they're nervous.'

'I think I'd be completely wrong.' Sally still felt stunned. What on earth had put the idea into his head? 'I'm not the sort of person who can hide my feelings. . .'

'I've never met a nurse yet who can't disguise what she's thinking. It goes with the job. Anyway, why would you need to?' He paused, lifting an eyebrow in question. 'Oh, I see. . . You're worried that you might show that you didn't approve?'

He was silent as he refilled both cups with fresh coffee, adding cream to his own, sliding the sugar bowl across the table towards her. She studied his hands as he did so. Long yet strong fingers, well-groomed nails. His movements were economical, not a gesture wasted, and she could easily picture him performing delicate surgery.

'I should think you would want, I don't know. . .

someone glamorous, with the right looks. . .'
Sally began.

'On the contrary. I want a person who's warm and
friendly, to give a more homely image.'

'Thanks a bunch. I've been called a few things in
my time, but never homely before,' Sally snorted.
'That's an American way of saying plain, isn't it?'

'You must know that I didn't mean that.' He took
a mouthful of coffee, staring at her above the rim of
his cup. 'Hazel eyes, glossy dark hair, legs that go on
for ever—how could anyone call you plain?'

'I didn't mean that I thought I was plain. . .I
meant. . .' Sally's voice trailed away in confusion.

'Whatever you meant, no false modesty, please. It's
an attribute I find particularly irritating.' He stared at
her once more. 'I think I should have said wholesome
rather than homely.'

'I'm not sure that I agree with the principle of
cosmetic surgery,' Sally protested, taken aback at his
unexpected comment. She was getting herself in a
tizzy, and no mistake.

'I'll bet you know nothing about it,' he said abruptly,
and she felt a *frisson* of nervousness at the way his
eyes flashed. Perhaps she'd better be quiet, for he
looked as though he could be pretty fierce if he lost
his temper.

'Sorry, I've no right to judge. As you can probably
tell, I wouldn't be at all suitable. In fact, I don't even
know why it's called "plastic surgery".'

'It has nothing to do with plastic, as such,' Neil
responded. 'It was a phrase first used by the Germans
in the nineteenth century to describe the moulding of

tissues. Not plastic, as we mean the word today.'

There was an awkward pause, and Sally fidgeted uncomfortably, feeling that she was being assessed by Neil's clear grey eyes and not enjoying the sensation at all.

'What exactly do you intend to do for a job?' he asked.

'I've not really thought about it.'

'You don't seem to have too many options available. You can't lift because of your neck injury; you told me that you'd handed in your notice, I don't know for what reason, and it seems to me that my offer is at least worth a try.'

He stared at the table, tracing a pattern with the edge of his spoon, his expression thoughtful; a downcast turn pulled the curve of his mouth into a tight line.

Sally's heart beat faster and she took a deep breath, her words coming in a rush. 'I don't want to work at a job because it's the final option.'

'Well, thanks very much.' Neil's mouth twisted wryly. 'I've never had an offer of mine called a "final option"! But at least you're honest.'

'Oh, please. I didn't mean to offend you.' Hastily Sally stretched across the table and lightly touched Neil's arm. 'You're right, I shouldn't make judgements on subjects I know nothing about and I'd be very grateful for a temporary post. Fair enough?'

'You've got a deal.'

Sally stiffened as he took her hand, but he merely gave it a brisk, businesslike shake, before beckoning to the waiter.

'I'm glad that's settled. Now, we'd better pay the

bill, and I'll take you home. You may be a lady of leisure at the present time and able to lay abed, but I've still got a lot to organise and have an early start planned.'

CHAPTER TWO

THE heavy Victorian frontage of the building, with its glossy black door, seemed overpowering, almost threatening, thought Sally, and it was scarcely lightened by the dusting of green on the horse-chestnut trees and the soft splash of colour from a flowerbed filled with bluebells spread in front of the window.

'Come on, I'll show you round the clinic and introduce any other staff that are here then, if we have time, perhaps we could go for a pub lunch.' Not waiting for an answer, Neil led the way up the three shallow marbled steps and pushed back the door, which squealed in protest as Sally followed.

'Hmm, front door needs oiling,' he muttered into a microcassette recorder, before replacing it in the outside pocket of his dark blue blazer.

Bewildered, she had to struggle to keep an interested expression on her face, remaining alert despite the rapidity of the day's happenings. Nagging doubts about her job still filled her waking thoughts and she'd been unable to sleep the previous night, wondering how on earth she would fit in. But it was too late to back down now.

Hurrying after Neil's long-legged stride into the wide hallway, she looked with interest at the curved staircase fronted by a large, clawfooted antique desk in sharp contrast to a modern, functional, green-painted filing cabinet.

The cornices edging the ceiling, the heavy chandelier that hung from the centre, the polished wooden banister, brought such an air of a bygone age that she wouldn't have been surprised to see a bustled figure sweep down the dark mahogany stairs, and the scent of beeswax and lavender polish added to the atmosphere.

'It still has a strong feel of the Victorian period, hasn't it?' Sally said softly.

'Do you think so?' Neil grinned appreciatively, his grey eyes alight with enthusiasm. 'I'm trying to keep it looking as unclinical—if there is such a word—as possible, to give the impression that the clients will be staying for a short break rather than coming in for what can be quite painful and traumatic surgery. This way.'

Almost impatiently he ushered Sally through a white-painted door into a corridor where the April sunshine poured golden light over rose-sprigged wallpaper, its dado of deep, rich blue exactly right—traditional yet modern at the same time. She felt her spirits lift as she entered.

'Did you have much work here to get the clinic set up?'

'Loads. It's important to me to get it exactly as I want.' He grinned. 'I'm a perfectionist, a hard taskmaster, as you'll discover, who expects the highest standards from my staff.'

Sally swallowed nervously.

'You don't have to look so worried,' Neil reassured her. 'Everyone gets at least a second chance after a mistake, but that's all. Right, here we are—the focal point of the clinic.'

Like a conjuror producing a rabbit from a hat, he swept open opaque glass doors that led into an operating theatre, a complete contrast to the Victorian ambience of everything they'd seen so far. It was as startling as a spaceship in a suburban garden—stainless steel fittings, a modern operating table, bright lights which provided a shadowless central work area.

Open-mouthed, Sally looked around, then moved to the cupboards lining one wall, gazing at the selection of instruments in it.

'I don't recognize any of these,' she muttered.

'Well, I don't actually use those.' Neil moved up behind her and stared over her shoulder. 'Those are part of my collection of early instruments, purely for show. That's a bistoury—a precursor of the scalpel, those are periosteal elevators—they were used for lifting the periosteum that covers bone, and that's an early trephine, for drilling holes in the skull.'

'Ugh.' Sally shuddered. 'I must admit, I thought they seemed a bit big for plastic surgery.' I hope Neil doesn't think I'm too much of an idiot, she thought, trying to read his expression. But he didn't appear to notice her embarrassment at her mistake.

'This is more the sort of thing we work with nowadays.' He took a pack from the top of a trolley and Sally gaped at the sight of the tiny forceps, scissors smaller than her finger, and needles with nylon thread that looked finer than a human hair.

'The needles don't look strong enough to pierce the softest silk, let alone skin. And how on earth can you see what you're doing with instruments as small as those?' she gasped.

'I have very good eyesight.' He studied her intently. 'And I can see that you aren't too sure about the job.' He put the pack to one side and tucked his hands in the pockets of his light coloured slacks, his eyes narrowed in contemplation.

'I'm fine, really I am,' Sally protested uncomfortably. Either he had the ability to read her mind, or she'd let her doubts show all too clearly. 'I must confess, I find it a bit. . .' she paused, aware that 'too perfect', the phrase that came to mind, might cause offence. 'I find the building rather overpowering,' she said quickly. 'And I'm still not sure that I'm the sort of person you need.'

'Feeling uncomfortable about the place is probably because it's empty. Just wait till we get the bustle of a normal working day, with Theatre lists and clients drifting around in their expensive night attire. It'll be a very different story then.' He reached forward and took her hand. 'And as for worrying that you might not be suitable, don't you trust my judgement?'

'Of course I do.' Trying not to show how his attention flustered her, Sally tried to pull her hand free in vain.

'Well, then, I am sure you'll do a marvellous job. So no more doubts, eh?'

'OK. I'll take your word for it. Could I see one or two of the rooms, do you think?'

Neil waited a moment, as though expecting some further comment, then shrugged. 'OK, let's go.'

There was a sound of hammering as they returned

to the hallway and climbed the stairs.

'Someone still working?' Sally raised her eyebrows in surprise.

'Yes, just one or two last-minute adjustments, but we'll be ready to open by tomorrow.

Neil led the way again, moving as smoothly as an athlete.

Wonder if he works out at the gym, or if that's just his normal way, Sally thought as she puffed alongside.

But she had no time to ask any questions, for just then Neil opened the door of a beautifully decorated bedroom—carpets, furniture and fittings all co-ordinated.

The window looked out from the back of the clinic, and Sally went across and stared down at the large garden, a chill air touching her skin and making her shiver as grey cloud built up, covering the only remaining patch of blue sky.

'A lovely garden,' she muttered, not knowing quite what to say about the room. Again, everything was too perfect, seemed part of a show, and didn't bear any relation to medicine as she knew it. It was difficult to imagine blood on those soft blue sheets, or someone daring to vomit in the luxurious bathroom.

'Well, what do you think?' Like a schoolboy with a good report, Neil waited in the open doorway.

'It's all absolutely beautiful, and I'm sure the clinic will be a huge success.' And she stifled her disappointment at the thought that Neil was, not wasting his expertise, exactly, but was somehow being too enthusiastic about superficial matters.

'I can see that you're still not too sure.' He took

her arm. 'As I said just now, it's always a bit depressing when places like this are empty. Let's go and get that lunch and I'll see if I can sort out some of your doubts.'

With exaggerated care, Sally tucked her bright green shirt into the waistband of her skirt and stepped behind the antique table that served as a reception desk.

'I didn't think I'd be this nervous,' she murmured to the empty foyer. Its black- and white-tiled floor shone, the soft green of the walls was soothing to the eye and the perfume from roses in cut-glass bowls on the window ledges reached her nostrils, but the calm and beauty of her surroundings weren't enough to settle her churning stomach. Hastily picking up her textbook for the umpteenth time, Sally flicked through the pages.

'I wish I knew more about plastic surgery,' she groaned softly, muttering the details she'd tried to commit to memory. 'Rhinoplasty, osteotomy, rotation flap, mammoplasty. Damn, I'll never get it right.'

She closed the book with an impatient slap of its red cover, and once again studied the appointment register, and the list of surgery for the week.

Any new job was nerve-racking, so it wasn't surprising that she should be apprehensive. Added to which, it was so different from anything she'd done before. Probably that was why she was worried; it wasn't that she so desperately wanted to impress Neil, of course.

'Deep breath, my girl,' she said sternly, suiting action to her words, then frowned doubtfully as Trish, the frighteningly capable secretary, appeared in the office doorway.

'Everything all right?' she asked. Sally nodded uncertainly. 'That's good.' Trish smiled reassuringly, then closed her door.

Sally took a deep breath. Compared with the other woman's duties hers were straightforward, for Trish, under Neil's direction, was responsible for arranging each patient's admission. Sally merely had to welcome them when they arrived, check that all the details in their files were correct, answer any queries, then take them to their rooms. But, simple though her job might appear, it would be easy to make mistakes. . .

'Don't be such a wimp,' she told her reflection sternly as she glanced in her small handbag mirror for a final check, pushing back her thick dark hair and smoothing on another layer of lip-gloss.

The colour of the blouse was a good choice, making her eyes look more green than hazel and emphasising the few auburn lights in her hair. Of course, everything would look a lot better without the wretched collar, she thought, but there wasn't anything she could do about that.

'I can't remember anything Neil told me,' she muttered desperately, thinking back to his lecture of the day before.

'Everything all right?' Startled at the unexpected sound of his voice as he repeated Trish's words, Sally looked up with a relief she couldn't disguise.

'Yes, thank you, nothing to worry about.' Hastily she crossed her fingers behind her back. 'I hope,' she muttered, praying that she would be able to cope with whatever the sunlit Monday morning had to offer.

'I'll be in my room if you need anything. Trish went through the appointments with you, didn't she?' He bent and looked over her shoulder at the open page on the desk and Sally, instead of reading the list of names, found herself studying his highly defined cheekbones and the shadow made by thick, straight lashes.

'Didn't she?' Neil repeated.

'Oh, yes, everything's quite clear.' Concentrate on what you're doing, Sally told herself sharply.

'Right. See you later.' He disappeared through the swing doors at the rear of the hall, his dark blue jacket snug across his shoulders, his strong athletic walk somehow incongruous in the confines of the expensively tailored suit.

But Sally had no more time to study Neil, for the first patient of the day—'Sorry—client,' she muttered under her breath—was coming through the front entrance.

She gazed fascinated at a sugar-pink mini-skirt, which barely covered the tops of legs that were nearly as long as her own.

'I'm Leanne Barton,' the new arrival said importantly, but her eyes flicked from side to side, betraying a nervousness that she was trying desperately to hide.

Suddenly very sorry for Mrs Barton, Sally smiled warmly. 'Ah, yes, we're expecting you.' She glanced at the small file in front of her. 'You've come in for a rhinoplasty, I believe.'

'A what?' The woman's heavily lipsticked mouth gaped in surprise.

'A reshaping of your nose,' Sally amended.

'Why didn't you say so the first time?' Mrs Barton's

voice was shrill. 'Instead of trying to frighten me with technical terms.'

'I'm terribly sorry. . .' Sally began.

'Where's Mr Lawrence?'

Oh, God, surely she doesn't want to complain about me, not my very first admission? So much for trying to show off my new knowledge, Sally groaned inwardly.

'I'm terribly sorry, Mrs Barton, I didn't mean to upset you. I'm afraid I'm not too used to the medical terminology myself, and merely said it as a reminder for my own benefit.'

'Well, all right, let's forget it.' Mrs Barton placed a small case at her feet and leant on the desk, tapping impatiently with nails the same bright pink colour as her suit. 'What's the procedure?'

'Well, Mrs Barton. . .'

'Oh, call me Leanne, please. "Mrs" makes me feel so old. It's not strictly accurate now, anyway.'

'Right, Leanne. I'll show you to your room, help you to get settled in, and take a few particulars, if I may. I know we have most of the details already, but there are one or two more facts we need.'

She bent and picked up the case, which thankfully was much lighter than it looked. 'Your room is on the ground floor and overlooks the garden. I think you'll find it comfortable.' Sally led the new arrival along the corridor, hopeful that her flow of words might help Leanne to relax.

'Oh, very nice.' Pushing back her permed blonde hair, the other woman went past Sally and stared around the room, smiling for the first time since her arrival.

'I'm glad you like it. This is the gold room and, as you can see, we've tried to make it as unlike a hospital room as possible.' 'We,' she thought, unable to control a grin. I've become very proprietorial all of a sudden. True to its name, the room was decorated in soft golds and yellows, the bedcover and curtains complementing the soft golden wood of the furniture.

Moving to an inset door, Leanne swung it back to look at the bathroom, large fluffy towels just visible through the gap.

'All right?' Sally raised her eyebrows.

'Yes, lovely.' Leanne flung herself into the small armchair and stretched her legs out in front of her.

'Take the weight off your feet,' she suggested, 'and fire away with those questions.'

'Well——' Sally picked up the file '—first of all, we need to know. . .' But before she could get any further there was a tap at the door, and it opened to reveal Neil's dark head as he peered through the gap.

'Mr Lawrence—Neil.' With one swift move, Leanne was out of her chair and smoothing the pink material of her skirt down over her hips.

'Good morning, Leanne. I just came to bid you welcome.' Neil held out his hand and shook Leanne's pink-tipped one. The pale blue stripes of his shirt emphasised his tan and Sally, looking at him from the corner of her eye, could well understand why the new arrival was fluttering her long false lashes. All his concentration was fixed on Leanne, as though she were the only person in the room, his magnetic eyes drawing Leanne's stunned gaze. He really is a charmer, Sally thought, sympathising with Leanne's reaction. She'd

reacted in much the same way at the restaurant, unable
to resist the full blaze of Neil's personality.

'Has Sally explained the operation to you?'

'I've not had a chance as yet,' Sally began.

'Right, let me show you these outlines. If you
remember, we drew them when you came for your
out-patient appointment.' He picked up the file, sat
on the edge of the bed, and gestured to Leanne to do
the same.

But an unexpected feeling that she didn't want Neil
to have everything his own way made Sally go to the
window. In the garden an elderly man she'd not seen
before was pushing a mower over the already smooth
grass. Its scent drifted into the room, bringing a fresh-
ness that helped to lighten the heaviness of Leanne's
musky perfume.

'I think we agreed that you only want a slight reshaping, to remove this small bump here and then
smooth out the line of the cartilage. Is that right?' Neil
spread a bundle of transparent sheets on the chair, the
thick black lines clearly visible against the gold of the
cushion. 'Just study these acetates, hold one over the
other, and you'll be able to see the full extent of
the operation.'

'There won't be any scarring, will there?' Leanne's
nervous fingers beat a tattoo on the edge of
the bed.

'Of course not. I wouldn't be doing my job properly
if I left a scar.' Neil laughed softly and squeezed the
woman's hand.

Sally turned and watched as Neil soothed all
Leanne's doubts. Talk about calming someone down,

she thought admiringly. He's better than any tablet from Pharmacy.

'I shall have to make a couple of small cuts here——' he traced the edge of Leanne's nostril with his forefinger '—then the rest of the reshaping will be done from the inside. You'll have a couple of nasty black eyes for a few days. . .'

'Wouldn't be the first time,' Leanne muttered.

Neil paused for a moment as Leanne fidgeted under his gaze, but didn't comment. 'Then, once the operation is finished, we'll put a small plaster splint on to keep the nose in shape.'

Sounds absolutely awful, thought Sally, frowning in sympathy.

'When the bruising's gone and the swelling has settled, I think you'll be very pleased.'

'When will you be doing the operation?'

'This afternoon, at about two o'clock. We did ask you in our letter not to eat or drink anything from six o'clock this morning, didn't we?'

Leanne nodded, her blonde hair swaying on top of her head like a miniature wheat-field.

'Good.' Neil took a stethoscope from his pocket. 'Now, any previous surgery? Any previous anaesthetics?'

'Nothing.'

'No allergies? No family history of diabetes, asthma, etcetera?'

'You asked me all this when I saw you at Outpatients.'

'I know, and I'm afraid Mike Henderson, our anaesthetist, will ask you again, but we can't be too careful.'

'It's not dangerous, is it?'

'Not in the slightest.' Once again Neil took hold of Leanne's hand. 'But any surgery carries a risk, and we aim to cut those risks to the absolute minimum. On second thoughts, I won't worry you with an examination now, because Mike will be here shortly.'

Sally studied him as he got to his feet, his lazy movements deceptively strong; she'd been listening with keen interest to the exchange between surgeon and patient, noticing the effect of Neil's smooth dark voice, the way Leanne was soothed by the surgeon's words, and shook her head in admiration.

'If you don't need me any more, I'd better get back to the desk. We have another client expected very soon. Nurse Simmonds will be coming to get you ready for surgery, Mrs Barton.'

Leanne wrinkled her soon to be reshaped nose as Sally patted her shoulder and hurried from the room.

'All right for some,' Sally muttered to herself, mentally comparing the reassuring way Neil had described the details of the operation with some of the hurried, poorly explained consultations she'd seen in the past.

Though that was hardly fair, she thought as she moved behind the reception desk and pulled out the file for the next arrival on the list. Neil was the sort of surgeon who would take the time and trouble to explain everything fully, even if he wasn't getting paid an enormous sum.

The rest of the morning passed quickly, though the contrast between her previous two posts—one on a busy medical ward and one in Coronary Care—and her present reception work couldn't have been greater.

She was surprised at how she began to enjoy meeting the clients, and also appreciated the time that she was able to give to each one. Neil also saw everyone, and Sally couldn't help a grin of admiration as each of the clients, male and female alike, hung on his every word.

By the time one o'clock came and Hilary the theatre sister arrived to get the operating theatre ready, Sally felt almost completely at ease in her new role.

'Have you had lunch?' Trish, her beautifully sculpted white hair and plain grey suit equally immaculate, stood at the reception desk as a longcase clock in the corner boomed out a sequence of Westminster chimes for one o'clock.

'No, and I must admit it's a long time since breakfast.' Sally grimaced hungrily.

'Don't wait to be told by Neil,' the secretary warned her. 'Just because he's barely human when he's working, he forgets that some of us have ordinary appetites that need to be satisfied. Come into the office; I think we can spare an hour.' She held open her door and ushered Sally through. 'I'll order some sandwiches and a pot of fresh coffee. There's a small staff dining-room, but I don't really want to leave the office as it's the first day; if we're here, we can be available should anything crop up.'

She swept papers from a circular table by the window. 'Bring up a chair while I ring the kitchen.' Trish smiled mischievously. 'They can't say that they're too busy to look after us today, for we have so few patients at the moment. We could have a proper meal, if you'd prefer?'

'Sandwiches are fine.' Sally set a chair by the table

and sank into it. 'I'm too excited to eat much anyway.'

'Right. Do you like paté?'

Sally nodded, then looked round curiously as Trish rang the kitchen with an order for paté, French bread, salad and a pot of coffee.

The office was purely functional, very different from the clients' rooms, and contrasted strongly with the smooth grandeur of the hall. A word processor almost filled the desk, and there was a fax machine, filing cabinets, and a tape recorder. The only touches of luxury were the thick, red-patterned carpet and a tilt-back armchair with a heap of cushions spilling from it.

Absently Sally settled herself more comfortably, and sniffed at a bowl of pink hyacinths in a ceramic bowl on the windowsill, enjoying the feel of the sun through the glass. 'Hark at that.' She tilted her head as a black-bird, perched on the branch of an ancient apple tree, poured out its heart in a series of liquid notes. 'It's so peaceful here it's difficult to believe that we're near the centre of town.'

'Only a few miles from the motorway as well, but you'd never know it. I think I'm going to enjoy being here rather than London. Gosh, it's warm.' Slipping off her jacket, Trish sat on the chair opposite Sally. 'Well, how have you found it this morning? Not too strange?'

'Not as I expected.' Sally grinned. 'But I've enjoyed it.'

Before she could say any more there was a tap at the door and a dark-haired waitress, her white overall gleaming, pushed open the door and set out a tray on the desk. The aroma of freshly brewed coffee mixed

with the spice of the paté brought grumbles of anticipatory hunger to Sally's stomach.

'Golly, I've just realized I'm starving. I can hardly
remember my morning branflakes.'

'We won't be able to manage this every day.' Trish
closed the door behind the waitress, then poured coffee
and passed one cup to Sally. 'You stay where you are.
I'll do the honours.' Deftly she set food on the two
plates, put plate and napkin on the small carved table
beside Sally and put her own meal on the far side.

'You said we wouldn't be able to do this every day.
Does it get much busier, then?'

Carefully Sally piled a knifeful of paté on to the
corner of her bread and bit into it eagerly.

'Well, the workload varies enormously, the same as
in hospital, of course. Today there are only a couple
of cases actually having surgery, so there won't be
much clearing up afterwards. You and I have the
heaviest load at the moment, with the paperwork. It
will take a bit of time to get a decent system going,
but——' she nodded reassuringly '—I know we can
manage very well.'

'I've never seen any actual plastic surgery; will I get
a chance to go to Theatre some time?' Sally asked,
and stirred thoughtfully at her coffee.

She wasn't that keen to see the surgery, but she
knew that she'd have to try and get to know all the
working facets of the clinic if she was to be able to do
her job properly. Even if it was temporary. And she
still wasn't too sure what her role was.

It was all very well for Neil to say that she was
supposed to reassure the patients—sorry, clients—she

told herself, but if she knew nothing about what went on in Theatre it would be difficult to do just that. She winced as she remembered her gaffe with Leanne! She'd hardly reassured her!

'Penny for them.' The other woman's words broke abruptly into Sally's reverie.

'To be truthful, I was wondering why Neil—Mr Lawrence, I mean—actually asked me to do this job. I'm sure there are dozens who would be far more suitable.'

'Didn't he tell you?'

Trish stood up and brushed crumbs from her lap into the wastepaper basket before covering the nearly empty tray with its white cloth.

'We. . .ell, he said that he didn't want some superior receptionist-type,' Sally began, 'but someone whole-some.' She grimaced. 'Makes me feel that all my overlay of sophistication has gone for nothing and that I must still look like the farmer's daughter I am.'

'I can guess why Neil picked you.' Trish studied her from shrewd dark eyes. 'It's because. . .'

'Did I hear my name mentioned?' The door flew open and Neil, a whirlwind in green theatre trousers and top partly covered by a white coat, came into the centre of the office.

'Now, why on earth should we be talking about you?' Trish teased.

'Can't think of anything more interesting, can you?' He spun on his heel, and winked at Sally.

'Come on,' Trish continued, 'what is it you want? I'm sure you haven't been parading in the corridors to give the clients a view of your operating outfit.'

'True. I don't usually show myself dressed like this,' he confided to a wide-eyed Sally. 'But I can't find an X-ray I need for Leanne Barton. Any ideas, Trish?'

The secretary frowned. 'You're sure it's not with her notes? I sent everything to Theatre this morning.'

'Oh, well, I'd better have another look. Perhaps Hilary has put them to one side. How did your first morning go?'

'Do you mean me?' stammered Sally.

'Of course. It's not exactly Trish's first morning. I won't say how long you've worked with me, Trish, so take that frown off your face.'

'I've enjoyed it, thank you,' Sally smiled.

'No problems? No doubts?'

'Not so far.'

'Good, I knew you'd be right for the job.' He glanced at the clock. 'Must get back to Theatre. Poor Leanne was nervous enough as it was, I'd hate to keep her waiting. See you later.'

'That was a bit disconcerting,' Sally muttered as Neil's broad back disappeared from view.

'In what way?' Trish sat behind the desk and took envelopes from a pile.

'Well, that Mr Lawrence should do his own errands. Wouldn't a surgeon normally send someone to fetch and carry for him?'

'Probably, but I expect he thought it would be quicker. He's always been one to do any job that's needed. Completely wedded to his work in all ways; probably that's why he's never married.'

'Well, I'd better get back.' Sally moved slowly to the door. There was so much more she wanted to ask about her new employer, but obviously now wasn't the right time.

Anyway, she was eager to start work again, a fact that surprised her. Perhaps her doubts about her suitability could be forgotten. Neil seemed certain he'd made the right choice and Trish had accepted her as a colleague, despite Sally's lack of experience.

Whistling softly under her breath, she left the office and happily returned to her desk. So far, so good, she thought, turning a dazzling smile on an elderly man who'd just limped through the front door and was heading towards her.

CHAPTER THREE

'IT AIN'T much but it's home,' Neil drawled, laughing at Sally's expression. She looked around, amazed as she studied the living-room of his house. The late evening sun streamed through a frame of plain white curtains behind him, encircling his head in a halo of light that, rather than making him look angelic, emphasised a devil's lift to his eyebrows. Dancing rays outlined his shape in maroon sweater and casual trousers, casting shadows over the furniture—two grape-dark settees and an armchair, their colour a sharp contrast to the white wool carpet. In one corner the gloss on the surface of a baby grand piano threw back a distorted reflection of her bemused stare.

'"Ain't much!" Is that remark meant to put me at my ease?' She breathed in the perfume of rose scented pot-pourri and looked round the room once more. 'It's a beautiful house.'

'I can't take all the credit for it. It was left to me by my grandmother, and a lot of the decorating ideas were hers. Anyway, do sit down. I should think you're pleased to get rid of that collar, aren't you?'

Nervously Sally smoothed at her neck, stroking the newly exposed skin. It still felt strange without the brace and she realized that she must appear stiff, the smooth athleticism in Neil's every move making her even more aware of her awkwardness. He took her hand, his long, clever fingers encompassing hers in a warm and friendly clasp, and ushered her forward.

'Take that doubtful expression off your face,' he ordered. 'What would you like to drink?'

'Anything that's colourless,' Sally said quickly, smoothing her coral-coloured skirt underneath her as she perched on the edge of one of the settees. 'Far from being doubtful, I think your home shows wonderful taste, but I must admit all that white wool makes me apprehensive.' She pointed down at the carpet. 'It would be just my luck to spill orange juice or a kir on it!'

'Hence the request for a colourless drink?' Neil smiled. 'No need for nerves. I thought we were friends as well as colleagues. Particularly with such a pleasant start at the trattoria.'

'Friends? Friends don't have this effect on me,' Sally muttered incredulously, but Neil didn't appear to have heard her. He turned towards a walnut sideboard and took glasses from the lower shelf.

'White wine?'

'With soda, please,' Sally murmured, clutching the glass firmly in both hands as Neil passed it to her.

'I'm not sure why you asked to meet me here, rather than at the clinic.' Taking a sip of her drink, she glanced up at him, before placing her glass on a small inlaid table at her side.

'Don't look so worried.' Neil's deep voice held a trace of laughter, but his expression was sober as he rested elegantly on the settee opposite. 'I merely wanted to ask what your plans are now that you've discarded your collar—how much physical stuff can you manage, do you have any other jobs in mind? That sort of thing.'

'Do you invite all your staff here for drinks and ask them about their work?'

'Sometimes.' Neil looked closely at her. 'Do relax. I don't bite, you know. To get back to what you were saying, I try to avoid interviews, consultations, et cetera at the clinic if I can. Anyway——' he gestured round the room '—this is much more pleasant, don't you agree?'

Maybe for you, Sally grimaced inwardly, a false smile glued to her face. Perhaps if she kept very still she wouldn't do anything disastrous. It was silly to feel nervous, for she had settled well at the clinic and, although Neil hadn't actually commented on her work, she didn't think she had made any errors.

'Well, have I given satisfaction so far?' The suggestiveness in her words didn't hit Sally for a moment, then she realized just what Neil's lazy grin implied. 'I. . .er. . .I . . . er. . .' Quickly, Sally seized her glass and gulped her drink, her creamy skin deepening to rose. 'I didn't mean. . .'

'I know exactly what you meant, no need to get in such a state,' Neil said in that voice that sent prickles through her. 'Do you have any ideas about your next move?'

She felt as flustered as a teenager on her first date. 'Obviously I'll finish the month in Reception, as we arranged. . .I thought you were about to tell me that I wasn't fitting in as well as you'd hoped,' she added abruptly.

'I wouldn't be going through all this rigmarole if that

were the case.' He frowned and shook his head. 'I'd
tell you, politely, of course, "I don't think this is working, how about calling it a day?" I'd do that with any
relationship, social or working.' He rested one foot on
the opposite knee, displaying a flash of navy silk sock
as he did so.

'So you're one of those people that believe in direct
speaking, whatever the circumstances?'

'I wouldn't say that.' His tone was impatient. 'Not
to the extent of hurting someone. But the reverse is
also true. I can't see much point in wasting a lot of
valuable time on matters that have no future. And that
applies in my work, as well.'

'So you think I've outlasted my usefulness?'

'I didn't suggest any such thing. I think you've fitted
in very well, despite your doubts at the beginning. But
obviously it was a stop-gap arrangement for you.' He
looked thoughtful. 'As a matter of interest, what
impressions have you received at the clinic so far?'

'One thing that has surprised me greatly is just how
many people lack self-esteem,' Sally murmured, com-
passion plain in her voice.

'Despite that, you still don't really approve of private
medicine, do you?' Neil lifted his glass, gazing at her
above the rim. The expression in his clear grey eyes
was unreadable, somehow in tune with the darkening
sky outside.

'Actually, I'm beginning to accept some aspects of
it. Especially in your field. But,' she added fiercely,
leaning forward, 'no one's health should depend on
their ability to pay. That was the whole object of the
NHS when it began—for everyone's care to be

assessed on need, not by the depth of the pocket.'

'Whoa, I'm not suggesting that it should be changed. I'm entirely in agreement with that principle, but. . .' He paused, obviously searching for the right words. 'But there are circumstances when it's all right to make a charge, surely?'

'Possibly,' Sally said grudgingly. 'But they are few and far between. I must say, I can't think of anything worse than undergoing surgery and having an operation when it's not medically necessary. . . It just shows how desperate the clients must be.'

Forgetting her earlier worry about spillages, Sally sat back on the deeply padded cushion of the settee. With a gasp of horror she saw her glass tip sideways, and a trickle of wine drip, as if in slow motion, from the edge of the table on to the carpet.

'I knew it, I just knew that would happen.' Feverishly she scrabbled in her bag for a tissue, but in a couple of long strides Neil was beside the table, dabbing at it with a snowy white handkerchief and had wiped the carpet dry before Sally could catch her breath.

'I'm so sorry.' Unthinking, she leant forward as he knelt beside her and rested an apologetic hand on his arm. But she withdrew it hastily, stunned at the iron-hard muscles beneath the smoothness of the wool and even more disturbed at her own reaction.

'For goodness' sake, relax.' He flashed her a reassuring smile, which displayed even white teeth, and patted her gently on the shoulder. 'You're as nervous as a kitten.'

Sally gave a tremulous smile, for it was true. She was

disconcerted by the discovery that she so desperately wanted to make a good impression. And her curiosity about her employer grew ever more acute as each day passed. But somehow he managed to keep the essential Neil hidden under a smooth veneer, making him difficult to assess, and she still found it hard to understand his apparent desire to make a profit with his surgical skills.

'Still, I suppose the incentive in nearly everyone's working life is the pay-packet. Why should he be different?' Unthinking, she muttered the words aloud, and felt a surge of embarrassment at Neil's questioning look.

'Pardon?'

'Nothing, nothing important.' Unable to think of anything to say, she sipped her drink. It was a pity she felt so awkward with him at the moment, for she had gradually become more at ease in his company. Starting with the trip to the restaurant after Jane's wedding and continuing at work they had found they had a lot in common, with a similar sense of humour, and conversation had been easy.

Somehow Neil had seemed so. . .not ordinary, exactly—no one of his height, six foot two if she was any judge, and with cool grey eyes that seemed to stare right through you, could appear ordinary—but he'd been very down to earth, yet excellent company. But the essential Neil, that she thought she was getting to know and like, was as elusive as quicksilver, sending her off-balance.

She studied him from under her lashes as he went and replenished her drink, then turned towards her.

'Well, at least I feel I know *you* a little better this evening. And I can understand that wholesome look you have, growing up on a farm.'

'Oh,' Sally groaned. 'You can't believe how I'd love to be thought of as ethereal just once, instead of being complimented on my bounding health. Still, I have to admit that the only time I've had off sick was with my neck injury.'

'Don't knock it. It's great to see someone as fit as yourself. For one thing, it's such a contrast to the people who figure so frequently in our working lives. Now, what were we saying?' He handed her the refilled glass and went back to his chair. 'Oh, yes, how about another evening out?'

'We never mentioned anything of the sort. And I'm not sure it's a good idea.' She sniffed pleasurably at the sweetness of her drink. 'I think it would be better if we stick to discussing work at the moment. It keeps things clearer in my mind.'

'Clearer in your mind? About what? Whether you approve of cosmetic surgery?'

'No, not that.'

'Well, then.' He stretched his legs out with a sigh. 'I know what it is—you're afraid that I might put pressure on you in some way.'

'I just feel. . .' She couldn't continue, for she didn't really know herself why she should be so wary of going out with Neil. 'I think I'd better consider another job pretty soon. Now that my neck has more or less re-covered, I'd like to get back to proper nursing.' She glanced up. 'If I'm not letting you down, of course. And, if there's nothing else to discuss, maybe I should be on my way.' Carefully putting her glass on the small table, Sally got to her feet.

'Sit down, do. You haven't anywhere special to go this evening, have you?' Neil's tone was impatient, but she could sense that he wasn't really annoyed. 'I want to know more about your reactions to what you've seen at the clinic.'

'But surely what I feel isn't important?'

'Perhaps it is. I think it's no bad thing to have some-one act as devil's advocate, to stop me becoming too complacent.'

'Oh, I don't think I can do that,' Sally began doubtfully.

'Afraid you'll hurt my feelings? I promise that you won't.'

'I don't want to be a devil's advocate, thank you.' She paused.

'Even if it would be a favour for me?' He grinned disarmingly.

Firmly Sally shook her head.

'All right then, what did you think of Leanne's operation?'

'I didn't see the actual surgery.'

'I realize that. I meant the results afterwards.'

'I was shocked by the bruising.' She thought back to how Leanne had looked, the discoloration that had developed over the next two days, the black eyes, the swelling, the plaster to keep the nose in shape, the difficulty Leanne had had in breathing through gauze packs in each nostril. Sally couldn't control a shudder.

'Everyone is a bit taken aback when they first see reconstructive surgery. Leanne had two lovely black

eyes, didn't she?' Neil smiled ruefully, obviously reading Sally's mind. 'Of course, something that is specific
to plastic surgery is the fact that all the damage is
visible. If I'd done an appendicectomy, or the removal
of gall bladder, for example, the immediate results
wouldn't show. But you can't hide a repair to a nose,
or a face-lift. That's one of the reasons that it's so
important to be very aware of the moral support our
clients need.'

'To be truthful, I couldn't see much wrong with
Leanne's nose before her surgery.' Sally stopped
abruptly. 'Sorry, that's not what you want to hear.'

'For goodness' sake!' Neil stretched towards her and
took her hand. 'Don't tell me anything, ever, do you
understand, just because you think it's what I want to
hear. I want the truth at all times, even if it isn't very
complimentary.' The intensity of his gaze seemed to
bore into Sally's innermost self as she stared back at
him. 'Do you know, when you're concentrating, your
eyes are almost the colour of butterscotch?'

Hastily Sally pulled her hand free. 'More "wholesome"?' she quipped, trying to stifle a blush.

'Don't be so defensive. It's fascinating.' Again he
looked into her eyes. 'Sorry, I shouldn't tease. But
it's tempting as you blush so easily. Anyway, back to
business. Leanne needed to have her nose reshaped,
not only for the physical change but because of the
psychological benefits.'

'In what way?' Absently Sally pulled at a loose
thread in her skirt.

'Did you hear her say that black eyes weren't a new
experience for her?'

'I think I did.'

'She's a gutsy lady, our Leanne. I won't go into all the details, but she was married to a man who used to beat her up; she wouldn't leave, though, because of the children. Reading between the lines, I gather he never mistreated them, only her.'

'That's terrible.'

'The children are old enough to be off her hands now, and she's seized the chance to be free of him. As well as a whole new wardrobe, new make-up, she decided that she wanted her nose fixed—part of the new image.' He paused and stared through the window at a cheeky thrush on a nearby branch, whose throat vibrated with the force of its song.

'Go on,' Sally encouraged.

'Maybe it's a bit fanciful, but I like to think that part of my job is to try and make dreams come true. I try to make the final results as perfect as possible.' He leant forward. 'And I defy you to find anything better.' He grinned, his teeth a flash of white in the darkening room as he switched on a brass table-lamp. 'If we can give the client what he or she is looking for, why should we say no?'

There was a pause, the silence broken only by the sound of the thrush still trilling in the garden.

'It's very peaceful here, isn't it? I can well under-stand why you wanted to move here from London. What started you in plastics anyway?'

'So you're avoiding a direct answer?' Neil grinned at Sally's embarrassed expression. 'It's all right, I don't mind. I've nothing to hide. Let me see, I did a short spell in ENT work, but it wasn't what I was looking for. But I found that I got a kick out of making sure that noses were in good shape after sinus operations, or surgery for a deviated septum. And that's how it all began. Not very interesting, is it? How about another glass of wine?'

'No, thank you.'

'Something to eat, perhaps?' Not waiting for her answer, Neil took a tray of sandwiches from the sideboard, and handed her a plate and napkin. 'Help yourself.'

'Someone's been busy.' Sally took one of the neatly cut smoked salmon triangles and bit into it enthusiastically.

'Do you know anything about how plastics started?'

Hastily Sally swallowed. 'No, nothing.'

'You must have heard of the Guinea-Pig Club, consisting of airmen who had suffered burns to their hands and faces during World War II?'

'I'm not sure.'

'Well, some techniques used in repairing war injuries are the basis of work done today. Of course, there was no such thing as microsurgery, and other advances have been huge, as in all branches of surgery, but a lot of the basic principles were there.'

I could listen to that voice all night, Sally thought, surreptitiously watching her companion's expressive face.

'Of course, plastic surgery goes even further back. Probably started in India, where noses were cut off as a punishment and doctors at the time attempted to replace them with tube grafts.' Neil sat back in his chair. 'Anyway, you must be getting bored with all this lecturing. That's not why I asked you to come here.' He ran impatient fingers through his thick dark hair. 'Have you any specific questions so far?'

Yes, thought Sally, leaning forward and taking another sandwich. Why is such an attractive man still unattached? Though that's not what he wants to hear! Quickly pushing the thought aside, she pondered for a moment, her sandwich forgotten.

'Do you ever have doubts about the ethics of doing cosmetic surgery?'

Neil blinked. 'Not really. I help people with my work, make the vast majority of them feel a lot better while improving their looks.'

'But they have to pay, of course. Where did Leanne get her money from, for example?'

'You can't seem to accept that it is quite ethical to charge someone for treatment, can you? I'd hoped that once you'd seen the work of the clinic some of your preconceptions would be put aside.' Neil's voice was suddenly cold. 'I'm not profiteering from Leanne's misery. I ask a very fair price for my expertise.'

'Oh, God, I didn't mean that. I would never presume. . .I meant, where did she get the money to leave her husband?' Sally added desperately. Embarrassed, she gabbled on. 'Anyway, aren't you prejudging how I think?'

'You've made your thoughts quite obvious, several times. Perhaps it's as well that you're planning to leave the clinic.'

Sally's heart sank. 'I apologize. I had no intention of criticising your standards.' Sitting upright, with her hands folded in her lap, Sally tried to look and sound professional. Her wretched tongue would get her into real trouble one day.

'It would be only fair that you finish the month, give us both time to make other arrangements, I suppose.' Neil's frown gradually eased, though there was still no warmth in his voice. 'Actually, Leanne won her money on the pools, and I can't think of a better way for her to use it than to set her life in order.' Smoothly he uncurled from his chair. 'Come on, I'll get you a taxi. My car is still off the road, and I'm afraid my young brother has reclaimed his old banger.'

'Oh, so it was your brother's car? I did wonder.' Recalling how incongruous a vehicle the car had seemed for Neil, at first she didn't register what he'd said. But as she stared up at the tall, powerful figure of her employer she suddenly realized that she was politely but firmly being shown the door.

'I've just remembered an appointment and will have to take a raincheck on the rest of the evening,' he continued, picking up the glasses and placing them on the sideboard.

'Oh, don't bother about a taxi if you're busy,' Sally said coolly, trying not to show how hurt she felt at Neil's dismissive tone. 'I can easily get a bus from the corner. The number fifteen goes right to the end of my road, so there's no need to put yourself out.'

'In that case, I'll walk you to the bus-stop.' He went swiftly from the room and reappeared with a jacket draped over one shoulder. 'Are you ready?'

'Of course.' With a toss of her head Sally moved past Neil in the doorway, not daring to look at his face. My God, but he was offended. Swallowing hard, she preceded him to the oak front door, standing aside as he opened it and ushered her into the gathering dusk, where the shrubs on either side of the drive filled the air with a mixture of flowery scents.

'There's no need for you to come with me.' She shrugged free from his escorting grip, shivering as his arm brushed against hers. 'I'm a big girl and can take care of myself.'

'I know you can.' He looked down at her from under dark eyebrows. 'But one who feels the cold, apparently. Put this on.' He slipped off his jacket and draped it over her shoulders. 'The evenings still get chilly, don't they?' he said in formal tones.

'Neil——' Sally stopped abruptly, her sandalled feet sliding on the gravel surface as she turned to face him. 'I was only trying to be honest. And you did ask me to act as devil's advocate, didn't you? I merely said. . .'

'I know. I'm pretty sensitive to criticism of my work.' He laughed softly. 'I really do have an appointment.'

'Well, in that case, don't let me keep you any longer.' Lengthening her stride, she set off at a fast rate through the wrought-iron gates into the lane that led to the main road, not looking to see if Neil was following her.

'Sally, Neil wants to see you. Can you pop along to his room, please?' Trish's voice, coming from her office, sounded friendly, but the summons was enough to set Sally's heart galloping at a rate that made her breathless. Was this the moment of truth? Was she about to be told that her job had finished? She had seen Neil only briefly that morning as he hurried past her desk calling a short 'good morning'. It had been impossible to tell if he was still upset by her words of the previous evening—ill-chosen, she had to admit.

Hastily combing her fingers through her hair, and smoothing on a bright slash of lipstick to give herself courage, she hurried to Neil's room and tapped on the door.

'Good morning.' He glanced up from a stack of papers and smiled encouragingly. 'Come and sit down.'

Warily she edged into the room, and went to the upright chair facing him.

'About last night,' she began, nervously twisting her hands together. 'I know I was out of order. . .'

'Yes, you were.' The timbre of his voice, if possible, seemed even deeper.

'I didn't mean to give offence, but you did ask for my opinion.'

He didn't answer, just gave her a searching glance. His suit jacket hung over the back of his chair and his pale blue shirt sat smoothly on his shoulders, the colour emphasising the tan of his skin, and subconsciously Sally breathed deeply at the scent of his aftershave. He was so attractive—all man, she thought.

'Anyway, I can guess why you want to see me,' she said hastily, scared of the way her thoughts were heading. 'I'm happy to stay for the rest of the month in Reception.'

'You're right in one respect. I do want to speak to you about your work.'

'Have I done something wrong?' Sally stammered.

'Not at all.' He settled himself more comfortably.

'You said you were keen to get back to real nursing. I wondered if you'd be interested in staying on here, combining Reception and some post-operative work?'

Sally stared at Neil, her mouth agape.

'I was under the impression that you're not too sure about me. . .'

'Rubbish,' Neil interrupted. 'I've seen how you deal with the clients—your warmth, your lovely smile. I realize that the workload is different from nursing in a general hospital, but it would be a way of getting back gradually, without putting too much strain on your neck.'

Sally swallowed, touched at the kindness of Neil's thought.

'If you think I can do it. . .' she began.

'Don't make up your mind immediately. Let me know when you've decided.'

'There's no need to think it over. I'd love to give it a try.' Sally beamed. So he still wanted her to say at the clinic. 'It's very kind of you. . .'

'Not really. I'm getting two for the price of one.' He grinned wickedly. 'Thus saving some of my vast profits.'

Sally blushed. 'I'm not going to be allowed to forget, am I?'

He leant forward, took her hand. 'Let's agree to differ and put our differences aside, shall we? My word, the skin of your hands is beautifully smooth and soft,' he murmured, studying her open palm. 'They're a nice shape as well. I'm not embarrassing you, am I?'

'Yes.' Quickly Sally pulled her hand free. 'What's the next move? I mean to do with work,' she added hastily as Neil took her other hand.

'What a spoilsport. Oh, well.' He sat back. 'The next thing is to get yourself kitted out with uniform dresses. You haven't any objection, I suppose?'

'No. But isn't a uniform too reminiscent of hospital?'

'Maybe, but it's practical. You surely don't want blood or worse on your own clothes, do you?'

Dumbly Sally shook her head.

'Let Trish know what we've arranged. You won't have to worry about the actual care, by the way. It's all very straightforward; we rarely operate on anyone who isn't basically fit. Zena Simmonds will be able to guide you, and I think she'll be pleased to have some help. Now. Back to work.' He got to his feet and held open the door, following Sally back to the foyer. 'Miss Maxwell should be here at any time. She's the seventy-year-old who had a hip replacement last year. Did you see her notes? The actual operation was a success, but she's not happy with the scarring. It restricts her hiking, would you believe, so I'm going to loosen the scar a little, make it more malleable.'

'Can't she have it done on the NHS?'

'Do you know, your mouth goes all pinched when you say things like that?' Neil's laughter was strained.

'Sorry. But why can't she?'

'If you must know, she prefers to pay, rather than use the limited resources of the NHS for something she says is largely vanity.'

'Hmm.'

'Shh, that looks like her now,' Neil warned.

Sally stared with interest at the tiny figure that pushed open the heavy wooden door. Barely five feet tall, with a mass of curly white hair, Miss Maxwell trotted towards the desk, a suitcase trailing behind her on wheels. Her motheaten grey coat was tightly buttoned despite the warmth of the April afternoon and one shoulder was weighed down by a brown leather bag that almost reached the floor.

'Let me take that for you.' Smoothly Neil lifted the case, and swung it easily beside the desk.

'Mr Lawrence, it isn't necessary for you to carry my luggage. Your hands are meant for finer things.' Her voice was surprisingly deep from such a small figure, and a bemused Sally had difficulty in concentrating on the routine questions before guiding the new arrival to her room.

'I'll carry this,' Neil said softly, his eyes dancing as they went to a pretty bedroom on the ground floor, with cream bedcover and curtains patterned with small blue flower. 'I can't wait to see how you cope with our Miss Maxwell.'

'Oh, very nice,' Miss Maxwell boomed, and Sally had to stifle a giggle.

'This is the bathroom——' hastily Sally opened the door '—and I hope you'll have enough wardrobe space. T.V. channels are listed here.'

'Never watch it. Such a waste of time. Young man, do you think you will be able to sort out this little problem for me?' Her jauntiness shrivelled in front of them, apprehension making her look her age.

'Of course I will.' Neil took her hand. 'I wouldn't have taken you on as a client if I'd thought otherwise.'

'Good. That's all right, then. Are you coming to watch, Nurse?'

'I'm not sure.' Sally blinked. 'But I'm sure I'll be with you afterwards,' she added, looking towards Neil for confirmation.

'That's true,' Neil reassured Miss Maxwell.

'Good. I'd like to think you were going to be there to wake up to. Got a good face.' Abruptly she leaned forward and patted Sally's cheek.

'Well, thank you.' Sally smiled, suddenly enchanted by the old lady.

'A very good face,' Neil echoed softly, his unexpected words lifting Sally's spirits. Obviously she'd been given a reprieve, and she intended to make sure that she didn't blot her copybook again.

'Well, Miss Maxwell——' she took the old lady's case '—let me help you unpack, then I'll organise a cup of tea.'

CHAPTER FOUR

'Oh, no, look at that! Filming some location work at Westleach, only a few miles from here, when it happened.' Sally passed the front page of the newspaper to Jane, her horror echoed by Jane's expression as the latter studied the headlines.

'"Melody Tranter". Is that her real name? "Beautiful young star of the. . ."' Jane murmured softly, skimming the words. '"Head-on crash, facial fractures. . ." God, just look at the state of the car! It's a miracle she got out of it alive!'

'I wonder if she'll be coming to us?' Sally called over her shoulder as she picked up their empty cups and took them to her tiny kitchenette.

'By "us", I take it that you mean Kynaston Clinic? What happened to your idea of packing it in?'

Sheepishly Sally looked at her friend. 'Neil asked me if I'd like to do some nursing and I accepted. As the duties are very light, he thought I could start off gently, not put too much strain on my neck.'

'I see.' Jane glanced at the newspaper once more. 'I doubt if even your wonderful Neil could manage to sort out the mess from a crash like that.'

'He's not my Neil,' Sally said sharply as she sank back on to the settee.

'Just wonderful, I gather.'

'Well, he's a superb surgeon, as you know.'

'How should I know?' Jane laughed softly.

'He's a close friend of Matthew's, isn't he?'

'Doesn't mean to say that I know how he operates.'

'Meaning?' Sally said sharply.

'Meaning nothing.' Jane giggled. 'You should just see your face. Come on, I'm only teasing. I'm thrilled that you've got something else organised. I should think the nursing will be much more to your liking than the reception work, anyway.'

Sally stretched out her long denim-clad legs. 'Probably, though I still have doubts about private medicine. I can't get used to the principle of people paying for treatment.'

'But if they pay their National Insurance and are then happy to pay again, does it matter? Anyway, with the cases that Neil operates on he's not exactly depriving needy patients of bed-space.'

'Have you been talking to him about this?' Sally stared suspiciously.

'No, why?'

'They're exactly the sorts of arguments that he uses.'

'Well, there you are, then. Anyway, to change the subject, life must be a lot more comfortable without that wretched collar—isn't it?' Gently Jane touched Sally's neck.

'Now that it's gone I can't believe I put up with it for so long. I still have to be careful about lifting, though. Just as well I'll be in a job that's not too demanding physically—no heavy patients.'

'What will you actually have to do?'

'Take care of the clients after their operations, particularly when they first come out of Theatre. With all

the surgery on the surface, if they get restless it's easy
for them to pull at dressings, or perhaps disturb the
suture lines, and apparently Neil doesn't like them too
heavily sedated post-operatively.'

'I should think you'll be much better off, rather than
going straight to a medical ward full of strokes. Just
think of all that lifting! To get back to this, though.'
Jane bent forward and retrieved the paper from the
floor. 'Melody Tranter is never going to regain
her looks.'

'Well, if anyone can repair her face, Neil can.'

'Back to wonderful Neil again, are we?' Jane's green
eyes were alight with mischief.

'Stop it. It's true, though, he's a marvellous surgeon.
I've only seen him operate once—well, not to actually
stay in Theatre. I popped in with some case-notes when
he was doing a Z-plasty.'

'A what?

'Z-plasty. It's when they make a zig-zag cut in the
skin, if scars have caused contractures, then fold the
points of the Z inside one another to lengthen the skin
area. The one that I saw was on the palm of a hand
that had been burnt.'

'It's what they do to loosen contractures after scarring, isn't it?'

'Yes.' Sally sighed dreamily. 'They say a surgeon
needs the hands of an artist, eyes like a hawk and the
patience of a saint, and it's got to be more applicable
in plastic surgery than anywhere. Neil says. . .'

'Neil says, Neil says. . . What else does Neil say?'
Jane muttered drily. 'And, by the way, have you heard
anything from Tom?'

Sally blinked at the abrupt change of topic. 'I have, as a matter of fact. After leaving me with the most casual of farewells——' Sally gritted her teeth '—he's had the nerve to send a postcard, and even phoned the other night.'

'Really?'

'Yes, really, And, typical of his selfishness, he forgot to check on the time difference between here and the States and woke me at three o'clock in the morning. Wasn't particularly apologetic, either.'

'Does Neil know about Tom?'

'There's nothing for Neil to know. Anyway, my private life has nothing to do with Neil. He's only my boss.'

'A boss who has taken you out to dinner. And didn't you say——' Jane emphasised with a jab of her forefinger in Sally's arm '—didn't you say that he is going to your parents' farm with you next weekend?'

'I thought he might like a complete change. And to be truthful, though he doesn't say much about his home-life, I get the impression that he's quite lonely. In that big house, all alone. Now that his brother is back at university.' Carefully Sally gazed ahead.

'Hmm.' Jane moved to the edge of her seat. 'Anyway, enough of Neil, fascinating though I'm sure he is; it's time to go. I intend to spend all my month's wages on a super new outfit, and this is the only afternoon that I'm completely free. Get your skates on.'

'It's all working out well, is it? You and Matthew?' Quickly Sally got to her feet.

'I couldn't be happier,' Jane said dreamily.

Sally stared with a momentary pang of envy. Jane

looked so at peace with herself, so complete, in contrast to the unnamed yearnings that had attacked Sally
of late, especially in the quiet reaches of the night.
She shrugged away the thoughts that were creeping
into her mind. 'And, like all happy newlyweds, I bet
you can't wait to get your friends paired off as well.
As long as you don't start on me,' she warned.

'Not even with the delectable Neil?'

'Don't be daft.' Hastily Sally turned away as she felt
the warmth colour her face. She had nothing to blush
about, for goodness' sake. Her relationship with Neil
was purely a working one, though she did seem to
spend a lot of time thinking about him, she had to
admit. She fretted over Jane's hints as she quickly
changed from her jeans into cool cotton trousers and
a green vest top.

'Come on.' Leading the way downstairs, Sally hurried Jane outside into the brilliantly lit morning,
pausing to breathe in the perfume of a yellow-flowered
broom bush in the garden. An unexpected feeling of
well-being swept through her, and she grinned as they
climbed into Jane's Mini and set off towards the shops.

Of course, her thoughts were full of Neil. He formed
a large part of her life; even if she wasn't actually in
his company she was at the clinic, with the stamp of
his personality evident everywhere. And what a personality. Maybe she didn't agree entirely with his work,
but his enthusiasm in everything he did certainly
carried all before it.

'But I shall concentrate on the shopping for the next
couple of hours.'

'Eh?' Jane gaped as she parked the Mini neatly

between a delivery truck and a Volvo.

'Nothing important.' Sally blushed. 'Just thinking aloud.'

'First sign of madness, they say, talking to yourself. Come on.'

Sally grimaced, then vowed again that all her attention would be on her friend, and wouldn't wander to a six feet tall muscular frame and cool grey eyes. . .

'Sally, can you come here a minute, please?' Neil's dark brown voice sounded abrupt, coming from the open door of his room at the clinic, and Sally pulled nervously at the waistband of her uniform dress as she went inside.

'How did you know it was me?' She smiled, gazing at Neil with unconscious longing as he sprawled in a leather chair, immaculate as always in stone-coloured trousers and a summer-weight jacket.

'Aha, I know everything about you.' He swung round to face her before she could lose her smile of delight at his unexpected words, teasing though they might have been.

'I'm very relieved to be able to tell you that there's a lot you still don't know,' she countered, closing the door behind her.

'What I don't know, I'll find out some time.' He gestured towards another chair. 'Sit down a minute. I want to talk to you.'

'That's sounds ominous.' Carefully Sally perched at the edge of her seat.

'Nothing to be nervous about.' He leaned forward and took a file from the low table between them. 'I only wanted to ask how you're getting on with the nursing side of things.'

'I haven't done much as yet. I'm doing the post-op care on a Robin Masters, and also Mrs Andrews, the face-lift booked for this afternoon, and Miss Maxwell is coming in later to have her stitches removed.'

'And you don't find it too much, doing some of the reception work as well?'

'No, I enjoy following the care of the client right through. And,' she said firmly, 'it's great to be back in uniform.'

'You prefer it? The grey stripe suits you, I must say.' He glanced approvingly across the room.

'Thank you. I know it's old-fashioned to like a uniform, but I feel it clarifies my role for the clients. In the nicest possible way, of course.' She glanced at Neil, suddenly aware that he'd gone quiet. 'Sorry, I do carry on a bit.'

'Not at all. It's all fascinating stuff. You're full of surprising observations, aren't you? I can't wait to see you on home ground at the farm.'

'I'm no different.'

'Well, you certainly seem to fit in well here.' He spun his chair again and looked towards her. 'Well?'

'Well, what?'

'If you want to stay on, we should regularise—dreadful word——' he laughed '——regularise your position. I take it that you're quite happy?'

'Of course.'

'As I said to you originally, nurses are past masters at disguising how they feel—part of the job. It could have been all play-acting,—your lovely smile, the way you welcome the clients and put them at their ease, your reassuring manner. . .'

'Whoa, you'll make me conceited. Though, of course——' Sally preened dramatically '—it's all true, I know that.'

Neil nodded, an appreciative glint in his eyes. 'Seriously, I've been very impressed. Would you consider a permanent post?'

Sally gazed at him, noticing the way the sun lit up his thick dark hair, the fine lines webbed at the corners of his eyes, the teasing look in his smile that made her curl inside.

'Ahem.' Quickly she cleared her throat. 'It's a bit too soon to decide. If you don't mind, I'd rather give it a longer trial.'

'Suit yourself.' Neil shrugged.

'Thank you. Now, I must get back to work before things get too busy.' Hope I haven't offended him, she worried, studying his rather stern expression as she got to her feet.

But, before she could escape, a tap at the door interrupted them. It swung wide to admit a stranger to Sally, the other woman's well-groomed elegance making Sally immediately aware of every smudge of mascara, every incipient spot she might have. Smooth, shining hair, black as a bird's wing, perfect figure hugged by a pale lemon suit, the newcomer, bringing with her a wave of musky perfume, hurried towards Neil as he hastily struggled from his chair.

'I've been waiting ages, Neil. You were supposed to pick me up, remember? Every time I tried to phone the line was engaged, so I've decided to come and drag you off in person. You did book a table for lunch, didn't you?'

Sally had never seen her employer so taken aback, his smooth good manners swamped by the new arrival.

'Sorry, Fiona. I won't say I forgot, exactly. . .'

'But you've been very busy, I know.' Fiona sighed. 'Are you able to come or not? There are a thousand and one details to organise for the ball and you did promise,' she wheedled, gazing intently into Neil's eyes.

Yuk, thought Sally scornfully. Fancy behaving in that childish way. She must be at least thirty-five. She stared resentfully, well aware of how jealousy was colouring her judgement. For Fiona was almost certainly no more than Sally's own middle twenties.

'I'll get back to work, Neil, if there's nothing else?'

'Sorry. Sally, this is Fiona Slingsby, an old friend. Fiona—one of my most treasured members of staff, Sally Chalmers.'

'How do you do?' Hastily Sally smoothed her palm on the side of her dress before shaking the other woman's outstretched hand with its garnish of red-painted nails.

'Perhaps we can finish our discussion later.' Neil smiled at her over Fiona's head and she could have sworn that there was a look of resignation on the surgeon's face as he ushered Fiona ahead of him into the corridor.

'Hmm,' Sally said grumpily. 'What a poser.' But she was honest enough to admit to herself that her annoyance wasn't wholly due to the fact that her time with Neil had been cut short. It had much more to do with Fiona's stunning good looks and easy swaying walk as she and Neil disappeared through the front door. Despite the little-girl voice, she was all woman.

'And you're not, I suppose,' Sally told her reflection after she made a small detour to the cloakroom, sent there by an unexpected urge to repair her make-up and tidy herself. She grimaced at the wayward strands of dark hair, the unadorned pallor of her skin.

'Oh, well——' she shrugged '—there's more to life than a beautiful face, I suppose.' But she knew her brave words were just that as she went back to the reception area and collected Mrs Andrews' charts, looking again at the photographs of the middle-aged woman.

'Sally, have you got a minute? Hello, what's the matter?' Trish clucked sympathetically as she studied Sally's forlorn expression. 'You look as though you'd lost a pound and found a penny.'

'Nothing's wrong,' Sally muttered, but her false smile didn't fool Trish who, without another word, seized Sally's arm and towed her into the office.

'Come on.'

'I've got to get Mrs Andrews' room ready,' Sally protested.

'We can spare the time for a cuppa, and you can tell me what's upset you.' The secretary went to the corner unit, filled the kettle and plugged it in. The rattle as she busied herself with mugs, tea-bags, milk and sugar allowed Sally to sit without speaking but, as soon as they'd settled with their drinks, Trish turned an enquiring look in Sally's direction. 'Now, why the long face out there? One of the clients upset you? Or has himself been telling you off?'

'Nothing like that,' Sally said hastily, studying the surface of her drink in an effort to try and escape Trish's penetrating gaze.

'You're not thinking of leaving, are you?' Trish took a quick swallow from her cup.

'No, in fact we were discussing a permanent post for me when. . .' Sally paused.

'When, what?'

'When some gorgeous woman called Fiona came and carted him off, leaving me very much in the air.'

'Not Fiona Slingsby?' Trish sighed.

'The very same. Why, do you know her?'

'I should say so. She's been trying to get her clutches into Neil for goodness knows how long. I don't think he's particularly interested, but. . .'

'Well, he went off to lunch with her happily enough,' Sally said gloomily, slouching back in her chair.

'You're not getting any ideas about him, are you?'

'Goodness! Of course not. I just wanted to sort out my job, nothing else.'

'As long as you're sure.' Trish stared intently before turning to the desk and picking up one of the folders. 'Well, if I'm any judge, you've no worries about work. Neil speaks very highly. . .Oh, excuse me, dratted phone. Hello, Kynaston Clinic, can I help you? Who did you say? Melody who?' Impatiently Trish gestured at Sally as the latter attempted to leave.

'Melody Tranter? That's right. I remember reading something about it in the paper. . .Yes, dreadful, dreadful. . .'

Not wanting to appear to be listening, Sally flicked through the pages of a journal, but her hearing seemed to be fine-tuned to the telephone conversation.

'He's not here at the moment,' Trish continued. 'He should be back at the clinic in about——' she glanced at the miniature clock on her desk '—in about an hour, I would say. Can I get him to ring you back? And your name is. . .?' She scribbled hastily. 'Right. I'll get Mr Lawrence to contact you this afternoon. Thank you for calling.'

She replaced the receiver and turned to Sally, her expression as alert as a terrier. 'Looks as though we might have the famous soap star Melody Tranter among our clientele. Did you read about her being injured in that road crash? Not that I ever watch *Friends and Lovers*, but. . .'

Is she coming here as a patient, then?' Her own worries forgotten, Sally stared wide-eyed at her companion.

'You're a fan, I take it?' Trish raised finely pencilled brows. 'Nothing has been decided, but I think it's a possibility, if Neil agrees.'

'Why shouldn't he?'

'He might not be too happy at the risk of the publicity.'

'But I would have thought publicity was good for business.'

Trish shook an admonishing finger. 'Don't let him ever catch you saying anything like that. This may be run as a business, but Neil's first consideration, whatever money might be involved, is whether he can actually do any good.'

Sally looked thoughtful. 'So in spite of this fancy clinic, he isn't after money for it's own sake, then?'

'Certainly not.'

'Of course I never thought he would take on a patient that he couldn't help. What will happen about Melody?'

'I should think she'll need a primary fixation of her fractures to start with. It sounds as though she has a Le Fort injury.'

'What's that?'

'I've got a write-up on it somewhere.' Pulling out the drawer of the filing cabinet, Trish flicked through the sections.

Intent on looking for the file, neither heard the door open and Sally, for one, nearly jumped out of her skin as Neil spoke.

'What are you doing back so soon? Not a very long lunch,' Trish murmured slyly, glancing over her shoulder.

'Now, Trish,' Neil warned. 'We bumped into Alan so I was let off the hook. After a quick coffee I left him and Fiona still arguing about the colour scheme for the ballroom.' He turned to Sally. 'What file is it you're looking for?'

Great, she thought, barely able to disguise her exhilaration that Neil had disposed of the gorgeous Miss Slingsby so quickly.

'Trish and I were discussing Melody Tranter's accident and I was asking about a Le Fort,' she answered crisply, determined to be the complete professional.

'Oh, yes, Melody Tranter.' Neil grimaced, his sensual mouth pulled into a narrow line. 'I've already spoken to her doctor. I'm not sure that I'm the best person to treat her. Judging by the medical photos, she has made a right mess of her face. Silly little madam—fancy driving like that in a powerful sports car.'

'You don't sound very sympathetic.' Sally sounded shocked.

'Of course I sympathise. She is only eighteen, bound to be intensely vulnerable about her appearance, and she probably feels even worse with her career depending on how she looks. But even so. . .' He sighed. 'I told the programme director I'll see her; he sounded as though he was on the verge of collapse himself.' Neil frowned with a shake of his head. 'And that was before I broke the news that she'll have to have a metal frame supporting her facial bones for at least four weeks.'

'Can you tell Sally about the Le Fort?'

'Oh, yes, come and sit here.' He stood behind an upright chair in the centre of the room, pushed Sally on to it and tilted her head so that she rested back against the smooth grey material of his jacket.

'There are three main severe bony injuries to the face,' he began. 'They are called a Le Fort One Two or Three, depending on the extent and the area. I think Melody probably has a Le Fort Two, which occurs when the fracture runs along this section here.' Gently he traced a line on Sally's cheek and upper lip with his forefinger. 'It follows the natural fissures of the connecting bones in the upper jaw, just at these points,' he continued, 'because when the face is

subjected to impacts these are the places most likely
to fracture.'

Sally sat rigid, scarcely able to breathe. Every move-
ment of his fingers sent trails of sensation through her,
like a series of small electric shocks.

'You'll never have need of my services,' he said
suddenly, looking intently at her. 'I've rarely felt such
lovely smooth skin.'

Sally's attempts at self-control nearly deserted her at
his words. During Neil's demonstration she had barely
taken in what he was saying, every part of her
desperate with longing to rest her face against the cool
skin of his palm. And the unexpected compliment sent
the colour flying to her face as she hastily got up from
the chair and went to stare from the window.

There was a moment's silence behind her, but she
didn't dare turn to face either Neil or Trish. She was
certain that all her longing must be written in her eyes,
that the attraction she felt was spelt on every freckle
she possessed.

Apparently unaware of how his touch had disturbed
her, making no comment on her sudden interest in
the view from the window, Neil spoke quietly to his
secretary.

'I think the reasons her director wants her here are
not only for the care and privacy but also to keep the
press well away. I don't know. The thought of reporters
hanging around. What's the matter, Sally, are you
cold?' For she had shivered as he moved up beside
her and rested a hand on her shoulder.

'No, just someone kicking my pot of ashes,' she
laughed, moving towards the door. Heavens, what was

the matter with her? A simple medical demonstration reducing her to melting point, for goodness' sake; it was only six weeks since Tom had left. She couldn't possibly be attracted to Neil so soon. Though there was no time-limit on attraction, if that was what it was.

Carefully she opened the door, anxious to creep away, when she realised that Neil had stopped speaking and was staring curiously at her.

'Are you all right? You're not sickening for the flu or something?'

'No, I feel great.'

'That's good. For a moment there you looked very odd.'

'Oh, thanks,' Sally muttered, hovering in the doorway.

'Don't be silly, I didn't mean that. I just thought you seemed a bit pale. Oh, by the way, can you spare me half an hour later?'

'Of course.'

'Good.' Neil turned to Trish. 'I've got Amanda Jackson coming in for review.' He frowned and shook his head. 'I don't know what I can tell her, so Sally can come and hold her hand—hold my hand too, if it comes to that.' He laughed at the startled expression on Sally's face. 'Don't look so disapproving. I'd like you to come to my room at two, OK?'

Sally nodded and closed the door behind her.

'"You seemed a bit pale",' she muttered, hurt at the comment. 'Anyone would seem pale when compared with the make-up Fiona was wearing.' And she tried to concentrate on the charts as she reached the desk, but not one word impinged on her fevered brain.

'Surely I'm not falling for him. . . Never,' she said
aloud, banging the beautifully polished desk with a
clenched fist. 'I swore I'd never get involved with anyone after that fiasco with Tom.'

'What's the matter?' Neil's laconic tones behind her
sent her into a fever of activity.

'Nothing. Just thinking aloud,' she murmured as she
hastily swept files into a heap, dropping several in her
flustered state.

'Well, if you're sure there's no problem.' Neil
retrieved the files from the floor, then leant against
the desk, his arms folded as he studied her, his elegant
figure completely at ease. 'Are you ready for that
appointment I mentioned?'

'Of course.'

'Right, then, let's go.' He moved with long strides
towards his room, Sally following close behind.

'I've not seen Miss—or is it Mrs?—Jackson before.
What's the matter with her?'

But Neil had no time to explain, for the client was
already waiting when they reached his room.

'Hello, Amanda, how are things?' Quickly he walked
towards the woman, taking her outstretched hand.
'This is Sally Chalmers, nurse-receptionist here.'

'How do you do?'

Through half-closed eyes, Sally studied the woman's
face as Neil started his examination.

'Amanda was burnt about four years ago and, as
you can see, her face has had a lot of grafting done
since then.'

Gently he held Amanda's chin, turning her face to
the light. Despite the scarring, she was unusually

attractive, with high cheekbones and a well-shaped chin. But the grafted skin was obvious—thickened white patches on the cheek, the corner of one eye puckered.

'This isn't my handiwork, but Amanda would like me to try and tidy it a little. Though I must say it all looks very satisfactory to me.'

'Can you do anything to improve it?' The woman spoke softly, her thick dark hair falling forward and partly shielding her face.

'I'm not sure I can make it better. What I would like to do is arrange an appointment for you to be shown how to use camouflage cosmetics with one of the Red Cross specialists. Then, if you're not happy with that, we'll review it again.'

'Have I really got to live with my face like this for the rest of my life?' Sally winced at the tremor in the other woman's voice.

'Amanda,' Neil said softly. 'Plastic surgeons aren't miracle workers, and this is very well done. Believe me, the scarring is minimal. I'd rather not carry out more surgery just for the sake of it. Would it help for me to arrange some counselling for you, as well?'

Amanda was silent for a moment, her fingers twisting her handkerchief into a ball.

'What do you think, Sally?' Neil turned to face her. 'Let's hear the woman's point of view.'

'That's a bit of an unfair question,' Sally muttered. 'But I think it's possibly better to try other options rather than have unnecessary surgery.' She leant forward and squeezed Amanda's hand. 'Why not give it a go? I think I would.'

'All right.' Amanda turned to Neil. 'I suppose I should thank you for being so honest, rather than spinning me a line.'

'As if I would.' Gently Neil brushed the scarred cheek with his fingers. 'I'll sort out those appointments, and Sally will get them in the post.'

'Thank you.' Swiftly Amanda got to her feet and left the room.

'Whew, I hate having to tell someone that there's no chance of making things better.'

'Well, you did it very tactfully. How was she burnt?'

'She slipped and fell into a bonfire and, unfortunately, was briefly knocked out.' He shivered. 'Anyway, thank you for your support.'

'I didn't do anything,' Sally said, bewildered. 'I don't really understand why you asked me to be present. Were you worried that she'd get very upset?'

'You don't realise how soothing you can be. It's one of your most endearing qualities, and a very useful attribute around some of the clients.' His grey eyes stared at her fondly.

Sally blinked, not too sure about the compliment, if that was what it was.

'Well, it's nice to be able to help.'

'Now, I must get on. I want everything straight before Saturday, as I shall be away next week.' He took her arm and turned her to face him. 'I'm dreadfully sorry, I'll have to miss our weekend. It's a shame. I was really looking forward to relaxing at your parents' farm. But—' he shrugged '—business must come first, and some dates have been unexpectedly changed.'

'That's all right.' Sally was surprised that she managed to sound so light-hearted, for her disappointment was enough to make her dizzy. Neil had made no previous mention of going away.

'I want to settle your contract before I go, so I'll see you this afternoon about that. Now, I've got to lift Mrs Andrews' face, and pin back young Robin Masters' ears.'

'Is that figuratively or literally?'

'Literally, of course. Robin is the ten-year-old we admitted yesterday evening, remember? Oh, I forgot, you were off-duty at the time. He's very self-conscious about his prominent ears, and isn't helped by the comments of his so-called friends—ears like taxi-doors, you know the sort of thing. His parents asked him what he wanted for his birthday and the poor little devil said an operation before he starts at his new school.'

Sally grimaced in sympathy. 'I remember, now. I read his file. I got the impression that he'd been pretty upset.'

'We'll sort it out.' Neil paused, staring intently at her. 'Sally, everything is all right?' Leaning forward, he took her hand. 'Once or twice, of late, I've thought you seemed a bit strained.'

'No, there's nothing wrong.' But her heartfelt sigh gave the lie to her words. For a long moment she stared back at him, her hazel eyes dreamy, her fair skin lightly dusted with rose. But, as Neil's magnetic gaze held hers, she was suddenly aware just how much her expression could betray and quickly pulled her hand free.

'Everything's fine, particularly now that I've

managed to get rid of my collar.' She picked up a folder.

'I'm glad to hear it. Are you coming to watch this afternoon? A nice straightforward introduction to reconstructive surgery—shouldn't make you faint or go green.' He stood back, a wicked light in his grey eyes, a mischievous tilt to his mouth.

'I've been a nurse for seven years, if you include my training——' Sally frowned '—and I'm not about to faint at the sight of a little blood.'

'I know you won't. We start at three and should be finished in good time to tie up our discussion. And I'll make sure that there aren't any interruptions from Fiona next time,' Neil added, his expression even more wicked as he strode off along the narrow corridor that led to the operating theatre.

CHAPTER FIVE

'You'll find Theatre greens to fit you in the women's changing-room.' Her fine blonde hair hidden under her cap, her stocky figure closely outlined by her tunic and trousers, Hilary pushed Sally gently through the doorway of the small cloakroom and pointed to a selection of theatre garb on the rail.

'When you're ready—clogs down there, by the way—come through the far door and stand quietly in the corner. Make sure you don't touch anything.'

I do know how to behave in an operating-theatre, Sally thought, her lower lip jutting resentfully as she slipped off her uniform and pulled on the shapeless outfit.

'Wish I hadn't shampooed my hair last night,' she grumbled, managing after a struggle to clip the wayward strands into her cap and pull the drawstring tight, before clip-clopping on wooden-soled clogs through the door indicated by Hilary. In the anaesthetic room a small figure lay full length on the trolley, thick lashes forming crescents against the pallor of his cheek as he drifted off to sleep.

'Can't see much wrong with those ears,' muttered Sally under her breath. 'Seems a bit drastic to operate.'

But as Mike, the anaesthetist, pushed the trolley into the theatre and lifted Robin on to the operating table she saw that the ears did, in fact, stick out almost at right angles on either side of the little boy's head.

She sniffed. The mixture of smells—antiseptic, the rubber of the wheels, the astringent overtones from the anaesthetic machine—all brought memories of her training days. Even the sounds were familiar—the squeak of the trolleys, the soft sigh of the ventilator, the clicking of wooden-soled shoes as Hilary set the instrument trolley.

Absorbed, Sally didn't notice Neil's arrival until he stood with his back towards her. Already scrubbed, he held his hands and arms in front of him.

'What's the matter?' Sally frowned.

'Could you tie my gown, please?' He glanced over his shoulder, grey eyes crinkling in amusement as she hastily slid her hands down the edge of the sterile gown and pulled the tapes free. She could just imagine his grin as he waited patiently, despite his mouth being hidden by his face mask.

Acutely aware of the slim yet powerful line of his body, she breathed deeply at the clean scent of his skin, now enhanced by the warmth of the operating-room. What was the matter with her? She'd seen plenty of partly clothed bodies before, for goodness sake. There was no need to blush and fumble like some lovesick teenager.

'Right,' Neil said briskly, oblivious to Sally's awkwardness as he snapped on rubber gloves. 'If you would like to stand here, you'll be able to see yet not be in the way. Everything all right at your end, Mike? If so, we'll make a start.'

The tall, slim anaesthetist nodded, pushing at his

glasses as he sat astride a stool near the head of the table.

'He's nicely asleep.'

'Good.' Neil hooked a foot under a second stool and dragged it near, then beckoned to Sally to move closer as he sat down, holding out his hand and taking the swabs soaked in antiseptic from Hilary before cleaning the skin thoroughly. Next, with a scalpel that was almost swallowed in his grasp, in one smooth action, he etched a shallow, crescent-shaped cut on the back surface of the ear, dabbing all the while at the tiny bleeding-points that appeared.

'If this was an adult, we could operate under a local anaesthetic, but with a child it's a lot nicer for him and easier for us if he's asleep during the operation.'

Sally watched, fascinated, as Neil made a series of tiny slashes in the cartilage, inking the outline with pin-points of blue dye.

'The next stage,' he told her, suiting action to the words, 'is to mould the ears into a better shape, then I'll suture the two edges of skin here, where I cut them at the start, put a dressing into the folds, then bandage it firmly to keep the ear close to the head.'

With a final snip of the scissors, Hilary cut the end of the fine nylon suture, before handing Neil gauze and bandages.

'How long will he have to stay at the clinic?' Sally asked as she rubbed at an itch on the sole of her foot.

'He'll probably go home after a couple of days, with the dressing to stay in place for about a week, then will need a bandage at night for about three weeks.'

'Isn't it a shame he was teased so badly?' Sally murmured sympathetically.

'Yes, it is. And the thought of having to face new people at his secondary school unnerved him completely.'

'Poor little chap. He looks so vulnerable with his legs sticking out from the bottom of the towels.'

Neil nodded in agreement, but was silent as he finally looked at Robin from the front to make sure that the ears balanced.

'Can you support his head for me, please, Sally, while I bandage him? We have to make it pretty tight, to keep the ears close to the head. Also to stop him pulling off the dressing if he's at all restless.'

Leaning her elbows on the edge of the table, Sally held Robin's head as asked.

'I use a continuous dissolving stitch for small children, as it means that they don't have to go through the trauma of having any sutures removed.' Neil chuckled as he peeled off his rubber gloves, untied his gown, and threw everything in the bin. 'Though it's funny how disappointed they are at the idea of having only one stitch—the greater the number of sutures, the greater the kudos, apparently. I have to reassure them that one very long stitch is worth far more than a lot of small ones.'

Sally grinned appreciatively.

'Thanks Mike, thanks Hilary. See you in a minute, Sally.' Neil nodded as he went through the swing doors, and Sally was surprised at how her inner glow seemed to disappear with him.

But she had no time to think about Neil, for the

young patient started to wake as Hilary and Mike lifted him from the operating-table to the stretcher.

'Are you looking after Master Masters?' Mike quipped, gently running a finger along the edge of Robin's eyelashes to test his level of consciousness.

'Yes.'

'Just go and get changed from your Theatre stuff, Mike and I will see you in Robin's room when you're ready,' Hilary ordered briskly, pushing the trolley into the corridor.

Swiftly Sally went to the cloakroom, peeled off the cotton trousers and tunic, slipped on her uniform and navy shoes, and hurried to Robin's room.

She wasn't unduly nervous, for the operation had gone smoothly. Apart from keeping a careful eye, in case Robin was sick, and making sure he didn't pull his dressings, she shouldn't have too much to do.

'Right, he's all yours.' Mike gave her a pleasant smile as Sally perched beside the bed, a receiver and towel on the cupboard top next to her. Intent on check-ing Robin's pulse and blood pressure—both normal, she was relieved to see—she didn't hear the door open behind her.

'Everything OK?' Light-footed as a cat, Neil came into the room and studied the small form on the bed.

'Yes, he's fine, observations normal,' Sally muttered softly, trying to control her suddenly racing heart.

'By the way, I've asked for coffee to be brought here. Thought maybe you could use a drink. If any blood oozes on to the bandage, let me know immedi-ately; other than that, there's nothing special to look out for. Now I must get back to Theatre for Mrs

Andrews.' He patted Sally lightly on the shoulder and left.

The touch of his hand, casual though it was, sent small tremors of sensation through to her fingertips.

'Just as though I've hit my funny-bone,' she muttered to the sleeping boy. 'But I don't think it's all that funny. I'm far too aware of him, you know.'

Taking a damp swab, she wiped Robin's forehead, then slid one finger under the edge of the bandage to make sure that it wasn't too tight. Everything was in order and she sat back in her seat, her thoughts drifting back to Neil. However hard she tried, she couldn't stop thinking about him. The attraction she felt had to be futile, for hadn't Trish explained that he was wedded to his work? And even if he weren't, there was the lovely Fiona very much on the scene.

Perhaps he's going away with her and that's why he's cancelled our weekend. Sally gulped, the thought scaring her insides. Perhaps his trip has nothing to do with work.

The thought was unbearable, bringing a sick sensation to her stomach. Gritting her teeth, she picked up Robin's file and read through the notes again. But even there Neil's distinctive handwriting, in the thick black ink he favoured, jumped off the page as a reminder of him.

'I thought I might join you for coffee. There's been a bit of a hold-up in Theatre. Mrs Andrews is too nervous to have her operation under local anaesthetic, so I'm just waiting for Mike to get her off to sleep.'

For a moment Sally wondered if her thoughts had conjured up Neil when he appeared, his Theatre gear partly covered by his white coat, a tray in front of him.

'How's the patient?' He smiled across at her from beside the window, leaning forward to place the drinks on an occasional table.

'He's fine. Still sleepy, though he opened his eyes a moment ago.' Sally blinked. 'It's nice of you to bring the coffee, but you shouldn't be waiting on me,' she protested.

'Call it a peace offering.' He poured coffee into two cups and handed one to her. 'I feel very badly that I've let you down over the weekend visit.'

Spooning sugar into his own cup, he sank back in the small armchair.

'That's all right. The arrangements weren't written on tablets of stone.' Sally shrugged. 'I'm sure there'll be other opportunities.'

'I'll hold you to that.' He yawned, the pinkness of his tongue clearly visible. 'Excuse me, I'm pretty tired. I was up till all hours, organising details for Fiona's charity ball. I shouldn't talk behind her back, but I know you'll be discreet.' He raised his eyebrows. 'Honestly, trying to discuss anything with her is like being under a waterfall in full spate. She enjoys pressure, but it's wearing if you're the recipient of her various instructions.'

So he was with Fiona last night, thought Sally as she sipped her coffee. Even nibbling at the sweetness of a chocolate biscuit did nothing to ease an unexpected ache in her heart.

'Have you known her long?' The glamorous brunette was the last subject Sally wanted to discuss, but as

Neil had mentioned Fiona it was difficult to avoid any reference to her.

'Our families have been friends for years. I knew Fiona when she was a spotty, gangly adolescent.'

'I can't believe she ever had a spot in her life.'

'She certainly did. Her complexion wasn't a patch on yours, none of that smooth creaminess.' He stirred at his cup and swallowed vigorously.

Sally couldn't hide how absurdly pleased she was at his words. 'It's a funny thing for a man to notice a woman's skin,' she muttered through a mouthful of crumbs.

'Not for me. It's part of my work to be aware of anything to do with appearance.'

They were silent then—Sally too stunned by Neil's compliment to be able to think of anything to say, Neil apparently lost in thought. An ambulance siren sounded in the distance, its rise and fall gradually slipping away, and the acrid smell of antiseptic drifted in through the partly open door. Neil sipped his coffee, gazing into the distance, his grey eyes crinkled like an old-fashioned seafarer's, looking for dangerous reefs ahead.

Did he have Fiona on his mind? Surreptitiously peering from under her lashes, her hazel eyes curious, Sally tried to guess. If he *was* thinking about the glamorous visitor of earlier, it wasn't a happy thought.

She drained her coffee and returned the cup to the tray, edging past Neil's outstretched legs. But she gasped and almost stumbled as he seized her arm and got up from his chair, turning her to face him.

'Sally, could I ask you a rather personal question?'

'What's that?' Sally stared back at him, noticing the shadowy depths of his eyes that gave nothing away.

'Do you disapprove very strongly. . .?' But just then they were interrupted by a retching noise, and Sally just managed to get a receiver by Robin in time to stop him from being sick over the bed.

'All right, it's all right, Robin,' Sally murmured, wiping his mouth with a tissue. 'I expect you feel better now that you've got rid of that lot, don't you?'

He nodded briefly, then turned his head on to the pillow and drifted off to sleep again.

'I must get back to Theatre. Mike should be more than ready by now.' With no reference to his words of a few minutes before, Neil hurried from the room, ignoring Sally's astonishment.

Frowning, she went into the *en suite* bathroom, rinsed out the receiver and returned to the bedside.

'What was all that about?' she muttered, intrigued. Neil's tone had been almost pleading. 'Do I strongly disapprove of. . . What?' She grinned ruefully. 'Fiona? Certainly. Of women surgeons? Never. Of cosmetic surgery? In some instances, I suppose I do. But that doesn't mean I disapprove of the surgeon.'

'Talking to yourself?' Zena Simmonds' dark curly head appeared round the door.

'Of course not,' Sally said stiffly. 'Talking to my sleepy friend here.'

'How is he?' The other nurse came into the room.

'He's fine, been sick once, but otherwise all right. Blood pressure, pulse and temperature normal.'

'Good. If he's sick again, give him some maxolon; it should stop his nausea. Will you be able to keep an eye on Mrs Andrews when she gets back from Theatre, as well as Robin? She's in the room next door.'

'Of course. Anything special I should do for her?'

'No, it's just that once she's properly awake she'll need to be nursed sitting up. To stop any risk of swelling in the skin that's been lifted. I'll be back anyway, before her op is finished. Now I'll let you get back to your solo chat.' Zena giggled at Sally's snort of disgust as she left.

But Sally had no more time to wonder about Neil's remarks, for again there was a knock at the door and Robin's mother appeared, her glasses reflecting the light from the window, the shoulders of her jacket dampened by spots of rain.

'How is he?'

'He's fine, Mrs Masters. Just been a bit sick, but otherwise everything has been very straightforward.'

'Mr Lawrence said I could come and sit with him, is that all right?'

'Of course. In fact, if you don't mind, I'll leave you to it for a bit, for I've another client to see to in the room next door.'

'I don't mind at all.' Mrs Masters slipped off her jacket, hung it on the door, and swiftly took Sally's place at the bedside. 'He looks surprisingly comfortable,' she murmured, gently smoothing the small area of Robin's hair that stood in a tuft outside the bandage.

'He does, doesn't he? Don't forget, if you need me, I'm only next door. And here's the buzzer to call for help, if you're at all worried.'

Sally placed the switch panel on the bed, then slipped quietly into the adjacent room. It looked as though everything had been set out ready for the patient's return from Theatre.

'I shall never think of them as "clients",' she muttered as she checked the bedclothes folded into a tidy pack in the centre of the bed, the portable suction in one corner of the room, receiver and tissues on the locker. If she was quick, there might be time for her to read up again on post-op care.

'"The most common complication is the development of a haematoma under the flap of skin. . ."' Hence the suction, Sally thought. Neil had explained that he would leave a drainage tube under the edge of the flap, so that any bleeding could be aspirated, and that sometimes a pressure bandage, similar to Robin's, was applied. 'Though that could be pretty difficult to keep in place, with an incision along the hairline,' Sally murmured, staring at the illustration.

'Ah, there you are. Neil wants you in his office,' Zena called from the corridor. 'I'll see to Dorothy Andrews.'

'What does he want?' Sally asked breathlessly.

'Didn't say. Don't look so worried,' Zena added kindly. 'He won't eat you.'

'Sorry to call you away.' Neil got up briefly from his chair as Sally hurried to his room. He looked as elegant as ever in a dark blue suit and crisp white shirt, his hair, still damp from his shower, brushed smoothly from his forehead. 'Sit down a minute. I've had a call about Melody; we're admitting her this afternoon. There's no skull or brain damage so they won't be keeping her at the General. Her studio bosses would like me to take over as soon as possible.'

'Well, that's very interesting, but why do you need to see me?' Sally straightened her belt and shifted more comfortably in her chair.

'I thought you ought to see the photos before she gets here, so that her face isn't too much of a shock. As you're new to plastics, I mean.' He took the file from the desk and passed it to her.

Heart thumping, Sally flicked it open. Don't be such a wimp, she told herself, ashamed of her nervousness, a few photos aren't a problem. But she couldn't prevent a small gasp of horror at the sight of the sharply delineated black and white pictures.

'Pretty terrible, aren't they?' Neil murmured sympathetically. 'You can see why I wanted you to have some warning.'

The face staring at her was scarcely recognisable as that of the vivacious teenage rebel Sally was so used to seeing on her television screen each week. Grazes and cuts painted smudges on the normally clear skin and the cheeks and jawline, well. . .

'Oh, that's terrible!' Involuntary tears started in her eyes.

'Hey, Sally, medical photos always emphasise the worst aspects. You mustn't get upset.' Neil moved smoothly from his chair and put an arm around her. 'Hey,' he said again. 'I didn't mean to shock you like that.'

Impatiently Sally brushed at the solitary tear that had escaped. 'Sorry,' she murmured gruffly. 'I just didn't expect it to be quite so bad. It's not only the cuts and abrasions, but her whole face is a completely different shape.' Frowning, she glanced at the page again.

'That's fairly typical of a Le Fort; like a rugby ball, isn't it? With all the front features flattened, so that the face is oval,' Neil explained.

'Will you be able to sort it out?' Turning towards him, her face only inches from his, Sally could see herself reflected in his clear grey irises. She gazed as if hypnotised while Neil gently thumbed away the tear on her cheek, then bent closer and lightly kissed her trembling mouth. It seemed an infinity of silence to Sally, broken only by the sound of her breathing and a rustling as she shifted in her chair.

'Sorry, but I couldn't help myself; you looked so woebegone,' Neil said softly, 'so unlike your normal self, that. . .' Clearing his throat, he moved back to his chair, staring keenly at her from under his brows.

'You look a bit stunned. . .'

'I'm sorry to be so. . .'

Their words clashed, dropping into an atmosphere that almost crackled with tension. Unable to continue, Sally placed the file on the table, hurriedly got to her feet, and went to the door.

'I'll see you later this afternoon when Melody arrives, shall I?' she called over her shoulder, as anxious now to escape Neil's presence as earlier she had been seeking it.

She didn't hear his muted reply, the words cut off by the closing of the door. As she hurried back to the reception area and collected Mrs Andrews' chart from underneath the desk, she couldn't stop her fingers

touching her lips to try to resurrect the sweet sensation
of Neil's mouth on hers.

But before she had time to work out the significance,
if any, of his kiss, the sound of an engine came through
the open front door, and Sally could see a white ambulance pull up outside. Melody Tranter? she thought. I
must be careful not to look shocked. Thank goodness
I saw those photos before she arrived.

She needn't have worried, for as the stretcher came
through the door, struggling over the temporary ramp,
all her professional skill came to the fore and her greeting was as down-to-earth as always.

'Hello, how do you feel after the journey? Not too
tired, I hope.' Taking the young girl's hand, Sally
smiled reassuringly, and was rewarded with a squeeze
from the newly arrived patient, the corners of her
swollen lips lifting in an attempt to answer Sally's greeting. In fact, despite her injuries, Melody seemed
calmer than the man who hovered beside the stretcher,
his pleasant, middle-aged face grey with concern.

'No problems on the journey?' Sally took the large
green envelope containing notes and X-rays from the
nurse escort and placed them on her desk.

'Nothing. All straightforward.' The other woman
nodded.

'That's good. The bedroom is on the ground floor.'

Sally held back the heavy fire door to allow the
ambulance men to push their trolley along the corridor.
With the skill of long practice they manoeuvred their
patient to the bedside, pulled back the duvet, and
carefully lifted her on to the bed.

'Comfortable?' one asked, smoothing the covers

over Melody's pyjama-clad figure.

'Yes, thank you.' The words were just audible.

'If you go through that door, there should be coffee available,' Sally called to the disappearing crew before turning to rearrange Melody's pillows. She beckoned to the man who hovered nervously outside the door.

'Now, Melody,' Sally began. 'I know it's difficult for you to talk, so I hope you won't think I'm being rude if I ask—your father, is it?'

'No, I'm the director, Paul Hughes.' His handshake was firm, but even so Sally could detect a slight tremor in his fingers.

'I'm Sally Chalmers—nurse, receptionist and general dogsbody.'

'Right. Melody's parents are in Florida, but we have contacted them and they're flying home today. I'll tell you anything I can. I've been with her ever since her admission after the accident.' Wearily he sank into the small armchair and leant his head back.

'You've arrived safely. Good.' Sally swung round at the familiar voice, her colour deepening momentarily as Neil entered the room, but after a scarcely perceptible nod of greeting all his attention was focused on the girl in the bed. Sally turned away, relieved that there was no hint in his manner of what had happened earlier. As if there would be, she told herself scornfully, before turning to listen to him, his deep, smooth voice immediately bringing an air of calm.

'First of all, do you remember the accident? Any idea at all?'

Melody shook her head before mumbling, 'The first thing I can remember is an ambulance man telling me not to move while he put a collar on me.'

'That was at the roadside?'

Steadily the questions continued, Neil sometimes asking Melody herself, sometimes turning to Paul. All the while they were talking his gaze was fixed on Melody's face, a reassuring smile lifting the corners of his mouth, all his concentration on the girl as though she were the only person in the room.

'I've tired you enough for today.' Briskly he stood upright. 'I think we might do the surgery tomorrow, if my anaesthetist agrees. He'll be along shortly to examine your heart and lungs. I'm going to have a word with Paul, then I'll come back and tell you exactly what's involved. Would you like something to drink?'

Melody shrugged.

'I take it that means "yes". Sally, could you get a glass of iced water? There should drinking straws in the kitchen.'

'Certainly. The notes and X-rays arc in Reception, when you need them.'

'Thanks, that's great.' Holding back the door, he ushered them from the room, then led Paul along the corridor towards Reception and Trish's office.

Apart from Melody's operation, the only other case listed was the removal under local anaesthetic of a mole which might or might not be malignant. But, in view of the length of time that Melody would be in Theatre, Sally thought it likely that the second operation would take place in the afternoon.

She checked through the notes, hearing the rise and fall of voices from Trish's office, curious to know what Melody's surgery would involve but too proud to ask to be included in the discussion.

'They might have asked me,' she muttered under her breath. 'After all, I bet I've watched her on television more than either of them.' Laughing at the idea that her viewing gave her special rights, she placed the notes for the next day on top of the desk and, suddenly remembering the promised drink of water, hurried to the kitchen for a jug and glass before returning to Melody's room.

'I've brought your. . . Whatever's the matter?' Sally stared in horror as she went in, the tray held carefully in front of her. For Melody was stretched out on the bed, facing towards the window, her shoulders shaking with painful sobs as discordant as a seagull's cry.

Quickly placing her burden on the locker, Sally rushed forward and gently put an arm around the sobbing girl.

'Melody, what is it? Who's upset you like this?'

Without a word the young patient reached under her pillow and produced a small hand-mirror.

'Oh, Melody. Oh, no. Is it the first time you've seen yourself since the accident?'

'I'm hideous, gross! Why didn't anyone warn me? I'll never be the same again.' The words, mangled by tears, were barely intelligible, but Sally understood only too well what Melody was trying to say.

'Neil! Thank goodness.' She looked up with a sigh of relief as the surgeon appeared. But she was stunned into silence at his horrified frown.

'Outside. I wish to talk to you in private,' he hissed. He pulled her none too gently from the room and spun her to face him. 'How dare you take it upon yourself to give that girl—that child—a mirror, before checking with me? Don't you realise it could put her psychological recovery back by months? You surely have enough sense to know that before anyone sees him or herself the right moment, the right person to explain is vital.'

'Now, just a minute.' At first too amazed at the unfairness of Neil's accusation, Sally just stared, aghast. Then, swiftly recovering, she took a deep breath. 'Before you jump to conclusions, perhaps you'd get your facts straight. I did *not* give that "child", as you call her, a mirror. She had one herself and I discovered her in that state. And might I add that you'd be better occupied dealing with her distress rather than jumping to misplaced conclusions about what *I* might have done.'

Flinging off his restraining hand, Sally stalked back towards the reception desk, blazing flags of temper alight in both cheeks. She couldn't believe it! From his comforting behaviour of earlier to suspecting her of doing something so stupid and so hurtful to Melody! She snatched up the phone from the desk and called Zena.

'I'm sorry,' Sally apologised. 'I've a splitting headache. Would it be all right if I go home early?' The part about the headache was true, her temper was now making her head throb painfully.

'Of course. Everything is more or less straight here.'

'Thanks.' Still seething, Sally tidied her desk, took her handbag from the small locked drawer, and hurried through the front door.

There were no more patients arriving that afternoon, and she would check again with Zena from home.

Anything to escape Neil until she'd had time to think things through.

'I'm not going to wait around for him to apologise, either, when he finds out the truth,' she muttered angrily as she switched on the ignition in her Metro.

The earlier showery weather had developed into a steady downpour, the overcast sky an apt reflection of her mood. Ignoring the clashing of her gears, she drove erratically but speedily from the clinic.

Her small flat had never seemed more of a haven as she hurried up the stairs, opened the front door and pushed up the enormous sash window. But the fresh air that gusted in did nothing to blow away her anger. Kicking off her shoes, Sally sank back on the settee and gazed into the distance, not noticing the scents stirred up by the rain from the garden below, the sweetness of the honeysuckle bringing the promise of early summer to the room, despite the rainy weather.

'Better ring Zena.' Pulling herself upright with a sigh that came from the depths, Sally picked up the old-fashioned telephone and quickly dialled the number.

'Hope Neil doesn't answer,' she muttered, crossing her fingers, and her wish was granted as Zena came to the phone.

'There's no need to worry,' Zena reiterated. 'I'm sorry you're not feeling well. Neil? No, I haven't seen him recently,' she continued, in answer to Sally's enquiry. 'He's busy with Melody, I gather. Do you want him to ring you?'

'No, thanks. And would you please not tell him I called?' Sally cut in hastily. 'I'll see you all tomorrow.'

Let him stew, she thought viciously, and if he doesn't
like it, he can lump it. Serve him right that I lost
my temper. But deep down she guessed that her next
meeting with Neil might be awkward, for he wouldn't
be impressed that she had driven home without
seeing him.

'Too bad,' she snorted as she clattered around in
her tiny kitchen. She put a tea-bag into a mug, added
boiling water and milk and cut a thick wedge of fruit-
cake, before returning to the sitting-room. 'I wasn't in
the wrong, *he* was, for jumping to conclusions, and
I'm not going to get my knickers in a twist.' Defiantly
biting a mouthful of cake, she picked up the local paper
and stared at the headlines. But the printed words
danced in front of her eyes as she tried not to admit
that her hero, the man she admired so much, could
have made such an error of judgement.

'Sally, open the door. I know you're there.' The rap-
ping of knuckles against the wooden panel echoed in
Sally's head like a drum, making her headache worse.

Dare I ignore him? Feverishly chewing a fingernail,
she hunched ever deeper into the cushions of her settee
as Neil began again.

'Sally, this is stupid. If you don't do as I ask,
I'll. . .I'll. . .just sit here, until your neighbours
wonder what's going on and your reputation is in
shreds.'

There was silence for a moment.

Despite the hurt she had suffered, Sally couldn't
control a nervous giggle. It was a bit silly, Neil camped
outside her flat, begging her to open the door. A

nervous smile on her face, she got up and tiptoed across the room.

'I asked Zena not to tell you I was here.' There was no reply. 'I don't know what you hope to gain by this,' she called softly. After all, she lived in the house and certainly didn't want the other occupants to hear her business.

'Sally, let's discuss things in a civilised manner.' Neil's voice had changed from pleading to peremptory.

'All right.' She pulled the door open so swiftly that he stumbled forward, seizing her arm in a grip of iron.

'Thank goodness you've seen sense.' Looking almost flustered, his dark hair falling forward over his face, a heavy frown lining his forehead, Neil straightened and stared at her.

'First of all, Zena didn't betray you. I saw your car leave and heard the last part of the telephone call. I guessed you hadn't truly got a headache.'

'I have got a headache and that's why I came home early.' Sally crossed to the centre of the room and gestured to the settee. 'Do sit down, you're making me nervous, looming over me like that.'

Did I really say that? She felt a whisper of gratification that Neil wasn't having things all his own way.

He looked stunned, moving to the settee without a word, all the while gazing at her as if she were a stranger. His grey eyes were shadowed, almost as though he was in pain, she thought.

'Would you like a coffee?'

'Have you got something cool? I came to see you in such a rush and. . .'

'How about a glass of iced water? Like Melody?'

'Ooh,' he breathed in sharply. 'That was a bit nasty. Please, at least let me apologise.'

Slowly Sally went and settled on the edge of an upright chair.

'Well?' she said shortly.

'I can't begin to say how sorry I am about the misunderstanding over Melody and the mirror. I should know you well enough by now to realise that you would never do anything so stupid.'

'It wasn't the fact that you assumed I didn't think, but that I didn't care. Did you forget that it was only a short time before that the sight of the photographs was enough to reduce me almost to tears? As if I would risk. . .'

'I know, I know. If you'll let me explain just why I'm so sensitive. . .' He paused. 'Could I have that cold drink? My throat is very dry; must be all the tension.'

'Just a minute.' Quickly Sally hurried to the kitchenette, made up some lemon barley water, and carried it through to the sitting-room, the ice cubes tinkling pleasantly.

'Thanks.' Not pausing for breath, Neil downed it in one go, placing the empty glass on the side-table.

'You certainly were thirsty,' Sally remarked.

'It's just that I want it out of the way.' He cleared his throat and sat back more comfortably on the settee, for the first time looking like the Neil she had come to know and. . . To know and. . .? Forget that, she thought.

'One of my first cases in plastic surgery in London was a seventeen-year-old girl who'd suffered severe facial injuries. She had soft tissue damage, consisting in the main of cuts and friction burns, plus one horrific laceration that ripped away part of the upper lip.'

Sally grimaced.

'I'd worked out how to do the repair, to cut a section from the fullness of the lower lip, rotate it into the gap left by the injury, with just a tiny connecting strip of tissue to get a good blood supply going in the new area until the new growth had taken. Then I would have severed the connecting strip. Unfortunately, her lip was too badly damaged to do a free flap graft—you know, taking arteries and nerves with the tissue and transferring them complete.'

'Microsurgery, you mean?'

'Yes. Anyway, I don't know who it was, but some-one lent her a mirror, and when she saw her reflection she tried to kill herself.'

'That's terrible.' Unthinking, Sally leaned forward and rested a hand on Neil's arm. 'What happened?'

'Oh, we managed to prevent the suicide attempt, but since then I've been ultra-careful that nothing like it should happen again.'

'I can understand now why you were so annoyed, but I'm still pretty hurt that you didn't trust me.'

'I'm a fool, and I hope you can forgive and forget.'

'I should apologise for losing my temper, I suppose.' Sally grinned wryly.

'Well, I must admit I was a bit taken aback. You've always been so calm before.' Neil chuckled. 'Your eyes were flashing with so much heat that I was expecting the fire alarm to go off at any moment.'

'Don't be silly.' Suddenly shy, Sally looked away,

unnerved by Neil in an apologetic frame of mind. Not that she expected it to last, but she couldn't resist the opportunity of prolonging the feeling of power it gave, even for a few minutes. So she kept a stern expression on her face, her mouth drawn tight, as Neil studied her warily. The look she returned was cool, for she wasn't about to make it too easy for him. 'Your apology is accepted, but please, get your facts straight another time. Has Melody recovered from the shock of seeing herself?'

'She was much calmer when I left. I managed to find a couple of "before and after" photos from previous cases, which helped to reassure her, and her parents should be getting to the clinic at any time now.' With a sigh of relief, Neil got up from the settee. 'I'm glad we've sorted everything out. As a peace offering, to show how I trust you, how about taking on Melody's post-operative care?' His earlier tone of apology had disappeared, his voice almost condescending now.

'Don't do me any favours,' she answered sharply, jumping up from her seat and walking to the window.

'What's the matter now? Are you determined to aggravate me?'

Sally didn't hear his approach, and the shock of his hands gripping her upper arms and turning her to face him was enough to make her gasp out loud.

'What are you. . .?' Her protest was stifled as Neil's mouth descended on hers. At first she was only conscious of pressure, but gradually his kiss softened, his hands sliding round to hold her close. She was lost in sensation, and at the same time acutely aware of the taste, the feel, the scent of Neil. As suddenly he released her, so that she staggered, off-balance physically and emotionally.

'Sorry,' he muttered. 'I don't know quite what happened there.'

Nor me, thought Sally, unaware of the depth of colour in her hazel eyes, the rose-red blush that had tinted her skin.

'That was a sneaky way of shutting me up,' she gulped, desperately trying to hide how stirred her feelings were by his embrace.

'I must get back.' Looking almost embarrassed, Neil pushed an impatient hand through his hair. 'I want to check on the facial splints we've had made. I might do the operation in two stages, to let some of the swelling go down before I finish it completely.' Buttoning his jacket, Neil brushed her cheek with his forefinger before hurrying from the room, his footsteps thudding down the thinly carpeted stairs and leaving a dazed and disturbed Sally behind him.

She breathed in the faint aroma of aftershave in the air, savouring the imprint of his visit for a long moment before hurrying to the bedroom. Edging round the bed, she gazed in the mirror.

'Sally Chalmers, I think he likes you! He was genuinely upset to know he'd hurt your feelings, and what about that kiss! What on earth brought that about?' she asked her reflection, unable to control a melon-slice grin of delight.

CHAPTER SIX

'WE'VE fixed Melody's fractures, can you see?' Neil pointed to the sleeping girl's upper jaw, where moulded splints covered her teeth and twists of wire kept the jaws in line.

Sally looked carefully. Being on a late shift, she'd not seen the actual surgery and now, with the results of the recently finished operation in front of her, she thought perhaps it was no bad thing. Though it would have been interesting, she could barely control a shiver as she imagined the grating noises made when the bones were manipulated into place.

As well as wires, small metal bars stood at right angles from Melody's forehead and cheekbones, with cross struts forming supports.

'How long will she have to have the splints?' Carefully Sally wiped a smear of blood from Melody's cheek.

'About four weeks. The immediate thing to watch out for is any vomiting, because with her jaws clamped together being sick is obviously a problem. That's why we keep wire-cutters at the bedside——' Neil gestured towards the tray on the locker '—and need that small spanner, in case any of the bolts have to be undone in a hurry.'

Sally swallowed nervously.

'Relax,' Neil reassured her. 'It happens very rarely,

but it's something to be aware of. Other than that, normal post-operative care—cleaning the mouth regularly, lubricating the wound sites where the supporting bars puncture the skin, encouraging drinks. Melody might well feel a bit claustrophobic when she first wakes up so, as well as maxolon to stop any nausea, I've prescribed a mild relaxant to calm her.' Yawning, Neil stretched his arms above his head. 'God, I'm tired now.' He was still wearing his Theatre clothes plus starched coat, the whiteness emphasising his tan, but no tan could disguise the shadows beneath his eyes.

'Never mind, no more operations today,' Sally said gently, almost overwhelmed by an urge to pull his head to her breast and give comfort. Hastily she turned and looked back at Melody, who was stirring and whimpering softly.

'I'll leave you to it. Sing out if you're at all worried.' With a reassuring wink, Neil left the room, leaving a very apprehensive Sally behind him.

'I'll do more than sing,' Sally said to the wooden doorframe. 'You'll hear my shout right down the corridor.'

She realigned the pillow at Melody's back, to keep her lying on her side, checked that the small red airway in her nose was clear, then sorted through the tray of implements.

'Wire-cutters, artery forceps, spanner for the bolts, suction catheters to clear her mouth. . .' Everything was complete and, unable to think of anything more she could do at the moment, Sally picked up the folder and read the operation notes. If anything, she thought, glancing at the sleeping girl, Melody looked worse than before, the bruises in sharp contrast to the pallor of her skin. And the ugly 'scaffolding' that supported the fractures! Well!

'Let's hope she doesn't get hold of a mirror with that lot,' Sally murmured. 'Goodness knows, I felt self-conscious enough with a surgical collar. That's ten times more disfiguring.'

But soon any possible reaction was the least of Sally's worries. It took all her ingenuity to stop Melody pulling at the splint as she gradually woke from the anaesthetic.

'Melody, don't pull at the frame,' she urged, for what seemed the umpteenth time, and turned with a sigh of relief as the door opened and Neil appeared.

'Hang on there, I'll get her some Omnopon.' He was back almost immediately with a wood-pulp tray containing two filled syringes.

'Some maxolon as well, in case the Omnopon makes her sick. I'll hold her while you do the honours.'

'Thanks,' muttered Sally drily, aiming with difficulty at Melody's threshing leg.

'Well done.' Slowly Neil released his hold, and stood back from the bed. 'If she's restless again, press the buzzer and someone will give you a hand.' He raised a quizzical eyebrow. 'Looks a mess at the moment, doesn't it?'

'Well, I suppose. . .'

'No need to be polite, but it will get much better, and surprisingly quickly, I promise. Now I must ring Mr and Mrs Tranter, then get my letters up to date. I'll look in again before I leave.' He sketched a small salute and disappeared.

The remainder of Sally's shift was peaceful, Melody sleeping quietly after the injections, showing no sign of her earlier restlessness.

'If you don't mind giving a hand, we can wash and settle Melody for the night,' the night nurse suggested as she arrived on duty later, her dark eyes glinting sympathetically at the sight of Melody's face.

'Of course, be glad to.'

Melody moaned as they sat her forward to pull off the pale blue Theatre gown and dress her in a baggy T-shirt, but quickly fell asleep again once they had finished.

'There, all comfortable. See you in the morning,' Sally called over her shoulder, slipping on her coat as she went towards the front door.

'God, you frightened me,' she gasped as a figure loomed in the dimly lit porch.

'Sorry, I didn't mean to,' Neil murmured. 'I was just on my way to see Melody, but I thought I'd let you know that I'll be going away earlier than I expected, from the day after tomorrow, in fact, so I'm going to be pretty busy until then.'

The fresh aroma of his cologne drifted towards her and she could sense him watching, even in the gloom of the rapidly approaching night.

'Well, thank you for telling me,' she said coolly, not betraying how his words made her spirits sink.

'I. . .I . . . thought you might be interested. It means I won't see much of you.'

'I understand. Have a good trip. Goodnight.' She was quite proud of her nonchalance as she hurried down the shallow steps and out to her waiting car.

Though she was puzzled as she drove home.

Perhaps he'd expected her to protest at the idea of his going away? Well, she hadn't any intention of betraying her feelings that much. Though how she would miss him, she thought, miss him desperately. He was becoming ever more important to her happiness, and it was something she would have to push firmly from her mind before bed, or she would never sleep.

But her worries were unfounded, for the long day took its toll and the early morning sun, its fingers creeping under the flowered curtains of her bedroom, was the first she knew after settling to sleep.

'I'm going to be late,' she muttered, showering and dressing in double-quick time, and driving to work without her usual wake-up cup of coffee. Throwing her coat at the rack in the cloakroom, she hurried along the corridor.

'How's Melody this morning?' Her cheery greeting broke off abruptly at the sight of Neil's grey-suited figure at the bedside.

'Good morning.' He didn't look up as she entered the room, and Sally said no more, just read the night nurse's report—anything to avoid looking directly at him.

'Had a good night, Melody?' Sally asked as Neil continued to ignore her. Poor little devil, her face looks ten times worse this morning. That puffiness, and those bruises around her jawline!

Melody nodded warily as Neil finished his examination, his fingers moving gently along the edge of the splint and checking the wires inside her mouth.

'All very satisfactory so far, Melody,' he smiled, going to the sink and washing his hands. 'Is your throat still sore?'

'Just a bit.' Melody's voice was an almost unintelligible gurgle, and again Sally felt overwhelmed with pity.

She placed a pad and pencil on the bed. 'If it's too difficult to talk, you can write what you want to tell me, Melody.'

Neil nodded, drying his hands and throwing the paper towel in the bin. 'Good idea. Do you need any more painkillers?' He paused at the end of the bed. 'No? You're sure? If you've any discomfort, tell Sally straight away, won't you?' He went to the door. 'See you later. Any problems, Sally, just call me. I'll be in my office.'

The day went slowly, for Melody dozed on and off, the intervals long enough for Sally to wish she had other patients to care for. And, apart from a flying visit at lunchtime, there was no sign of Neil. And his absence made the day even emptier as it progressed.

'How long will Neil be away?' Carefully avoiding Trish's watchful gaze, Sally sorted the charts, the white rectangles of stiffened paper resembling a wayward pack of cards. Two days since Neil had gone she didn't know where, and the early summer sun seemed to have lost its warmth; the birds, busy mating and building nests in the horse-chestnut outside, aroused her interest not at all, and the sweet scents of the wallflowers had mysteriously disappeared, all gone in a feeling of loss that frightened her with its intensity.

She thought back to his departure, his goodbye friendly but casual.

'It's not the best time to be leaving Melody.' He had frowned as he packed his briefcase with a selection of reports, along with a favourite needle-holder and an instrument pack from Theatre.

'Must be important to call you away,' Sally had muttered, trying to disguise how lost she felt at the idea of Neil's absence.

'I'm afraid it's something that can't be postponed. But I know you'll take good care of Melody, and Pete Thompson, a colleague, is available for any emergency call-outs.' And Neil had hurried to the front door, Sally trailing in his wake, as she had told herself afterwards, like some disconsolate puppy.

But she had been fractionally comforted by his unexpected hug before she waved to the departing car from the main door of the clinic.

It hadn't helped her that Neil had told her no more about his trip, merely reiterating that it was business— business that included Hilary and Mike. Nor had Trish given any explanation, and pride had refused to let Sally pump the secretary for information. Pride, and also a worry that she might betray how much she missed their boss.

Now Trish's agile fingers travelled over the word processor keyboard before she replied.

'Four or five days all told, providing there are no hitches.'

'It must be important for him to leave Melody so soon after her operation.'

'Yes, it is,' Trish answered in a non-committal tone.

'Anyway, there's not a lot more he can do for Melody at present. Until some of that swelling goes down all she needs is careful nursing and lots of moral support. And she's getting that from you.'

'From me?'

'With the way she's taken to you, Neil realised he was leaving her in good hands.'

Sally clipped the charts together, moved to the window, and stared into the garden. 'She does seem to like my company, I suppose. Thank goodness some of the puffiness has gone from her eyes. She was panicking badly yesterday, because she couldn't see out of her left eye.'

'But you managed to reassure her?'

'I think so, though it's still difficult to understand what she says.'

Trish sighed and flexed her fingers. 'Do you fancy a cup of tea?'

'The universal panacea,' Sally murmured softly, listening to the rattle of cups behind her as Trish set out the tea things.

'And chocolate cake, as well? Nothing like a good dose of chocolate to lift the spirits.'

'I'd love some. Then I must get back to Melody; the physiotherapist should have finished with her by now.'

'Eat up,' Trish ordered. 'You're lucky—no worries about your figure.' She stared admiringly at Sally's tall, lissom frame.

'Glad someone appreciates me. Neil always says so much about my wholesome appearance that I feel like a milch cow.'

'Don't be silly; I'm sure he doesn't picture you like that.'

'Well, when I see some of the model-types that come to the clinic. . .' Sally paused.

'Mere clothes-horses, not real women.'

'Why do clichés give so little comfort?'

'I don't know.' Trish stared at her, her pleasant face curious. 'Tea's ready. Help yourself to. . . Oh——' She broke off in mid-sentence. 'Come in,' she called in answer to the knock at the door.

'Is Sally with you? Ah, Sally, any chance you can get back to Melody?' Zena Simmonds appeared in the doorway.

'Is there something wrong?' Quickly Sally put her cup on the tray.

'She's just a bit fed up,' the other nurse answered. 'Can't say I blame her; her parents aren't able to visit today and the television producer. . .'

'Paul, do you mean?'

'Yes, that's him, he won't let her have any other visitors while she's got that face frame on.'

'I'll come straight away.' Sally glanced at Trish. 'Thanks for the tea.'

'And sympathy,' Trish murmured to her disappearing back, but Sally was already hurrying along the corridor to Melody's room.

'Hi.' There was no reply to her cheerful greeting, but Sally saw a flicker of interest as Melody looked with her one open eye, the other still closed by swelling from the operation. 'How did physiotherapy go?'

'All right. God, I'm fed up,' the younger girl moaned through her splinted mouth.

Gently Sally closed the door behind her. 'Let's do your mouth-care, then how about a short stroll out in the garden?'

'Can I do that?'

'I don't see why not. It's not your legs they've operated on, is it?'

Wordlessly Melody shook her head.

'Right, then. Mouth-care first.' Sally opened the paper-wrapped pack, set out swabs and lotion in small gallipots, and put the tray on the bedside table.

'I hate this.' Frowning as much as she was able, Melody leaned back against the pillow. 'Do I have to have that horrible-tasting mouthwash?'

''Fraid so,' Sally said briskly. 'It's the best one there is for cutting the risk of infection.'

'I thought the antibiotics did that. I'm like a pin-cushion with all the jabs.'

'Well, they're important as well. Don't forget, there's always a chance of debris getting in the wound at a road accident.' While she was talking Sally dabbed the small pink sponge into the mouthwash, slid it between Melody's lips, and brushed it along the line of her upper gums, taking care not to catch the swab on the black nylon sutures inside Melody's mouth. She repeated the action, gradually covering all the inside surfaces.

'Right, Melody, just some Vaseline for your lips, antiseptic ointment on the wound-sites. . .'

'What wound-sites?' muttered the young patient nervously.

'Where the rods of the metal frame puncture the skin.'

'Do those bars go into the bone?'

'Just enough to support the fractures,' Sally explained. 'They are just a sort of splint.' Delicately she finished the treatment by smoothing clear gel on Melody's skin.

'How does that feel?'

'Much more comfortable.' Melody sat forward and managed a lop-sided grin. 'Now, as I've been such a good patient, how about that walk in the garden?'

'You're on.' Relieved at the apparent improvement in Melody's mood, Sally quickly cleared away the mouth-care tray, washed her hands, and went to the door.

'I think a wheelchair might be sensible until we get outside, then you can see how you feel. After all, it's not long since the operation.'

'You're the boss.' Hastily Melody seized the blue dressing-gown from the bottom of the bed, swung her legs out over the edge and fumbled her feet into a pair of mules.

'Take it steady,' Sally warned as she hurried into the corridor and brought back a lightweight wheel-chair. 'You might be giddy.'

But Melody's eagerness could bear no delay. She was in the chair almost before Sally had fixed the retaining clips in place.

'Right, I'm yours to command.' Sally edged through the doorway, along the corridor, and through the rear porch on to a paved area outside.

Melody was silent for a moment, breathing deeply at the perfumed air. 'That sun feels marvellous. But I'll have to manage without my lovely new shades,' she giggled, pointing to her eyes.

'Beautiful out here, isn't it?' Sally pushed her patient towards a wooden seat at the far side of the lawn. 'Let's sit here for a bit, then perhaps you can have a walk if you feel up to it.'

They rested in silence, Melody staring round at the flowering shrubs, the white candles on the horse-chestnut tree, the brave colours of the wallflowers in the beds.

'I feel almost human,' she sighed, swinging her slippered foot out in front of her.

'Good. Feel up to some exercise?'

Taking Melody by the arm, Sally helped her to stand and, after a moment to get her balance, Melody set off firmly along the gravel path that edged the lawn.

'Bet Neil would have a fit if he saw me now.' She giggled again.

'I should think he'd be delighted to know you were feeling well enough to try out your legs,' Sally said sharply, holding Melody's elbow in a supportive grip.

'He's gorgeous, isn't he?' Melody said wistfully.

'Certainly is,' Sally agreed fervently, her thoughts as full of longing as Melody's voice.

'You quite fancy him, don't you?' Melody glanced from the corner of her swollen eye.

'Not at all, ours is purely a working relationship.'

God, were her feelings that obvious? For fancy Neil she did, in fact, she more than fancied him, if truth were told. 'Right,' Sally said crisply, 'I think that's far enough for one day.' Firmly she ushered her patient towards the garden seat and lowered her on to it. 'There you are, you did very well,' Sally encouraged. 'Now what would you like to do?'

'Just relax here, if you can spare the time.' Melody closed her eyes and lifted her face heavenwards. 'I love the sun. I'd like to be on a beach right now, somewhere like the West Indies, without all this on my face, of course.' She was silent for a moment. 'I sometimes wonder if I'll ever get back to normal.'

'Now, Melody, no negative thoughts. Trust Neil. He'll get your looks back, I promise.' Gently Sally squeezed her hand.

'I can't believe I'll ever get rid of this lot.' Impatiently the younger girl pulled her hand free from Sally's and tapped the edge of the frame. 'It's not fair; I wasn't driving that fast.' Tears welled from the swollen lids and trickled slowly towards Melody's chin.

'Come on, I'm supposed to be cheering you up. I'll get the sack if I don't do better than this,' Sally joked.

'Where's Neil? I wish he was here.'

'So do I, Melody, so do I,' Sally muttered softly. He'd been so pleasant, so friendly since their argument, that she had almost begun to hope at least for *some* return of her feelings.

But, lo and behold, a couple of days later, he had gone without so much as a word of explanation, and she knew no more of how he felt than when they had first met at Jane's wedding. She couldn't kid herself that a pleasant kiss had been. . .

The call from the porch doorway was like a reprieve and Sally looked across and saw the smiling faces of Melody's parents; it was difficult not to sigh out loud as they hurried towards them.

'How's my little girl?'

Tenderly Melody's father rested his hand on

Melody's head before sitting on the seat beside them.

'Delighted to see you both.' Sally got to her feet. 'I'll be back later, Melody. Just going to organise some tea.' She glanced at Mrs Tranter, receiving a smile which didn't remove her frown—a permanent fixture these days, on an otherwise pleasant face.

Must be worse at times for them, Sally thought as she went inside and rang the kitchen for tea to be sent to Melody's room later. Seeing someone you loved in pain must be more difficult to bear than your own suffering.

She collected the admissions book from the desk and looked through the list of patients. It was no good; she still couldn't get used to the idea of calling them 'clients'.

But, despite her fierce concentration, thoughts of Neil kept intruding, images of his face superimposed on the words in front of her. She could picture clearly the way his mouth lifted at the corner when he started to laugh, how his face lit up as he talked about his work; she could hear the deep, bitter-chocolate sound of his voice in her head so vividly that it was difficult to believe he was nowhere near.

She welcomed the interruption when the front door flew open and Miss Maxwell's chirpy figure appeared.

'Come to have my dressing changed,' she called. 'Got a walking holiday planned next week, so need to be as mobile as possible.'

'Come to the treatment-room and I'll have a look,' Sally invited. 'How have you been getting on?'

'Marvellous,' the elderly lady boomed. 'That boy-friend of yours deserves a medal.'

'My boyfriend! He's not my boyfriend; he's my boss.' Sally opened the door of the small dressing-room and helped Miss Maxwell on to the couch.

'Well, you could have fooled me,' the old lady remarked as she pulled up her skirt and lay on her side.

Not answering, Sally carefully peeled off the sticky tape and removed the gauze. Apart from some reddening along the suture line, which would soon fade, the wound had healed completely, all the puckering from the previous scar gone.

'It's fine. No need for anything else on it. Just go home and have a nice warm bath.'

'Wonderful thought.' Miss Maxwell pulled her dress straight and slid from the couch.

'Er, Miss Maxwell, before you go, do you mind telling me. . .?' Sally's voice faded as she tried to think of a suitable way of asking the question in the forefront of her mind.

'Do I mind telling you what, my dear?'

'What gave you the idea that Neil—Mr Lawrence, sorry—is my boyfriend?'

'Ah, do I detect a spark of interest in those lovely eyes? I've always been sharp to notice things.' She patted Sally's hand. 'And the pair of you have a certain look. I don't know how else to describe it. Not wrong, am I?'

Sally was silent, unable to think of a reply. Just the fevered imaginings of an elderly lady, she told herself. But the glow that lit her inside as she ushered Miss Maxwell to the front door was enough to warm her for the remainder of her shift and throughout the drive to her parents' farm.

CHAPTER SEVEN

'GUESS who?'

Sally's cry of delight echoed in the hallway as fingers covered her eyes, a body stood close behind her and words were softly whispered in her ear.

'Neil, you. . .Tom! What are you doing here?' Dumbfounded, she stared at Tom's smiling face, inches from her own.

'I've come to visit my girl.' A small frown of annoyance creased his brow, the skin stretched tight and reddened by the sun.

'Your girl, indeed!' Swiftly Sally went to the reception desk and sat firmly in her chair. Trying hard to stifle a feeling of overwhelming disappointment, she ignored the petulant expression on Tom's face.

'My girl,' he repeated. 'I'm home for a couple of weeks' leave and I thought you'd be pleased to see me. Don't tell me otherwise; I know you're pretending.' He leant across the desk and planted a noisy kiss on her hastily averted cheek.

'Well, thanks,' he grumbled, tucking his khaki shirt more firmly into the waistband of his jeans. 'I've just travelled three thousand-odd miles, the first person I call to see—not even bothering to get over jet-lag—is you, and you're as warm as damp sea-mist.'

Funny how she'd never noticed in the past just how

sulky he could look, Sally thought, trying hard to smile a welcome.

'By the way, who's Neil?'

'Neil? My boss, Neil Lawrence, why?'

'That was the name you called out. . .'

'I called out? You must have made a mistake.'

'I know what I heard. You said. . .'

'Well, if that's true, your curiosity needn't worry you any longer,' Sally cut in. 'You can meet him right now.' Her heart began a slow thud of anticipation at the sight of the car pulling to a halt on the gravel front outside.

He looks tired, she thought, studying Neil's face greedily as he strolled through the front door, his light blue shirt and summer trousers emphasising the lean lines of his body, the tan of his skin darkened since he'd been away.

'Hi, Sally, how's my girl?'

She blushed, embarrassed in front of Tom at Neil's using the same phrase in greeting.

'I'm hardly "your girl",' she said hastily, looking sidelong at Tom's knowing expression.

'That's a shame. Still, I live in hope.' He said no more, just glanced curiously at Tom for a moment, then set his briefcase on the floor beside the desk before bending forward to kiss her lightly on the mouth.

'Everything's under control,' she said breathlessly. Except me, she thought, trying not to show her surprise at the unexpected gesture. 'Did you have a good trip?' Gosh, she'd missed him so.

'Fine, but busy. How's our patient?'

Again he glanced at Tom, his keen eyes raking the

length of the other man who stood, arms folded, watching the exchange between Sally and Neil with interest.

'She's improving slowly, still pretty fed up. Oh, by the way, Neil, this is an old friend, Tom Monroe. Tom—my employer, Neil Lawrence.' Both men eyed each other warily as they shook hands, then Neil retrieved his case and moved swiftly towards the office.

'I'll catch up with the rest of the details from Trish. Could you be an angel, Sally, and organise coffee for us? Nice to have met you.' He nodded curtly to Tom, closing the office door behind him.

'How about organising some coffee for me while you're about it, Sally?' Tom leaned over the desk. 'So that's "Neil",' he whispered. 'It looks as though I've got a rival. What's his line of work?'

'How did you know I was working here?' frowned Sally, ignoring Tom's words. 'I didn't get the job until after you'd left.'

'Rang your parents, looking for you, if you must know. They told me.'

'And they didn't tell you what sort of clinic it is?'

'No. Nothing unsavoury, is it?'

'Of course it's not. Don't be stupid. Neil is a plastic surgeon. . .'

'Hmm, plenty of money coming in then, can see why you prefer him to me. Lots of rich old women looking for the secret of eternal youth, eh?'

'It's nothing like that. The cases he operates on are very varied, why, only last week he——' Quickly she bit off the words, horrified at how nearly she'd betrayed Melody's presence at the clinic.

'I must get the coffee.' Frowning, she hurried

towards the kitchen. Had Tom been this crass when she had known him before? For goodness sake, they had gone out together for nearly two years, though it was hard to imagine, seeing the way he had behaved since he arrived. Or was it perhaps the contrast with Neil that showed Tom in such an unflattering light? Hastily she collected a tray of coffee and returned to Reception, looking round carefully but to her relief Tom was nowhere in sight.

'Never thought the day would come when I'd be glad to see the back of him,' she told herself ruefully, aware again of her embarrassment in his company, particularly with Neil there.

She tapped on the office door and went in with the steaming coffee, its aroma preceding her.

'I'd rather not say anything to her as yet——' Neil broke off abruptly as she appeared.

'Oh, thanks, Sally, that's the best thing I've smelled all week.'

He took the tray from her and set it on the table by the the window. 'Are you able to join us, or do you have to get back to work?'

'I've no admissions until after eleven.' She tried not to seem too eager as Neil gestured towards the swivel armchair.

'In that case take a pew; I'll catch up with your news once Trish has finished her report.'

'Sally is more *au fait* with what's been going on outside this office than I am.' Trish took her cup and sat behind the desk. Her grey hair, swept back today in a severe bun at her neck, conversely made her appear younger.

'You look a bit tired.' Sally stared up at Neil. 'Was it a hectic conference?'

'Conference? Oh, yes, conference. Very busy. Actually, I must go and see Melody before anything else crops up, but first I'd like to know how she's been while I was away.' Speedily he drained his cup and set it back on the tray. 'Come with me, Sally, and fill in any details I should know about.'

Barely giving her time to finish her coffee, he ushered her through the door, retrieving his briefcase and swinging it lightly as they walked along the ground floor corridor to his room.

'Not many patients for you to see, actually.' She hoped she sounded more professional than she felt. Almost horrified at the delight that had surged through her on seeing Neil, she could scarcely concentrate.

'Well, let's see Melody first, shall we? And I gather Robin is coming in for his check-up.'

'And there are two admissions booked: a lady for excision of surplus tissue from the abdomen after losing five stones in weight, the other a man——' Sally's voice lifted in surprise '—for blepharoplasty.'

'Tightening of the bags under his eyes, eh? You seem surprised. What's wrong with a man wanting to make himself look better? A wish to improve one's appearance isn't solely a female prerogative.'

'No, I realise that. But men have a distinct advantage when it comes to getting older—they just tend to look more distinguished.'

Neil laughed. 'Do they? I hadn't noticed. Anyway, I'm sure John Whitton's self-esteem, if nothing else, will be helped by his operation. Now, how does Melody seem psychologically?' Neil spoke softly as they opened the door to Melody's room.

'Pretty good, all things considered. She missed you, though.'

'That's nice. Did you miss me?'

'We all missed you,' Sally said primly. 'Don't start fishing for compliments. You know the place is nothing like the same without you.'

He chuckled softly. 'Don't give anything away, will you? I'm not afraid to say I missed you—missed you a lot more than I thought I would.'

'Did you?' Sally gulped. 'Nice of you to say so.'

'Not nice at all, it happens to be true.' Gently he flicked her upturned chin with his finger. 'In fact, thoughts of you had a habit of intruding when I least expected. . .'

'We'd better get on,' Sally said breathlessly, scarcely able to believe her ears; she would have to ponder on Neil's words when she had more time, but still her heart sang a jubilant song. 'Morning, Melody.'

The teenager turned to face her visitors, her swollen eyes now open enough to peer at them both.

'About time, Doctor.' But although her words were abrupt, she seemed more up-beat than she had been since her operation. Neil's magic presence again, Sally thought. If he can make me feel good just by being here, and I'm fit, how much more will he affect Melody? She pulled a chair to the bedside and handed Neil a pencil torch for him to examine his handiwork.

'That's looking better, much better.' Holding her chin, he tilted Melody's face towards the window. 'Mmm, the swelling's gone down, hasn't it? How are you managing with food and drinks?'

'Slops, more slops, and a filthy taste in my mouth, which doesn't help my appetite,' Melody grumbled. 'And Sally keeps giving me "mouth-care" as she calls it.'

'Which is very necessary and prevents any infection,' Neil said sharply.

'What wouldn't I give for a hamburger with at least a pint of tomato ketchup splattered all over it?' Melody pulled impatiently at the neck of her outsize T-shirt, distorting the clown's face on the front. 'I still look worse than this, don't I?'

'I'm not going to tell you any lies.' Neil perched on the edge of the bed. 'You've still got a way to go, but every day is a step nearer to getting your looks back to normal.'

'I believe you. Sally said the same thing. She said that you're the sort of surgeon that can work miracles, that you've got magic hands, that. . .'

'I don't think Neil wants to hear all that now, Melody,' Sally cut in sharply. Every inch of her skin prickled with embarrassment as Neil gazed at her, a speculative glint in his eyes. Blast Melody, Sally thought to herself. Usually you have to strain to understand what she's saying, now every word is crystal clear.

'Magic hands, eh?' Neil chuckled softly, splaying his fingers out in front of him. 'Interesting thought. Anyway, Melody, one piece of good news. You can go home for a few days.'

'Great! Can Sally come with me?'

'That might be a little difficult to arrange. We'll have

to see how busy the clinic is likely to be. How do you feel about it, Sally?'

'I don't mind, if I can be spared.'

'Possibly to get Melody settled in. What time will your parents be here, Melody?'

'About two this afternoon.' Like a small child, Melody clapped her hands.

'You'll have to remain in the house or your own garden, of course. No visiting friends,' Neil warned.

'I wouldn't want to, looking like this.' Melody's voice was horrified.

'That's OK, then. We'll be back in a minute.' Neil paused. 'Can I speak to you, Sally?'

Giving Melody's hand a squeeze, Sally hurried after him, but had to stop abruptly as he turned to face her.

He took her arm, studying her intently, his expression sober.

'What's the matter? Are you worried about Melody? She's much brighter, you know.' Sally laughed. 'What a mixture, though. A world-weary young sophisticate one minute, then behaving like a three-year-old, the next.'

'This has nothing to do with Melody. She's improved enormously, I agree, but actually I want to ask you a favour.' Gently Neil pushed back a strand of her hair with his finger, letting his hand stay for a moment on her neck. In the dimly lit corridor, his half closed eyes were dark shadows, the thick straight lashes shielding his thoughts.

Sally swallowed nervously, aware of the butterfly kiss of his breath on her cheek, the clean fresh scent of his skin, the cool strength of his hand, now resting on her shoulder. Taking a deep breath, she managed to control the tremor that ran through her at his touch.

'Is something the matter? I'm quite happy to go with Melody, if that's what worrying you.'

'That's not the problem. I'm trying to ask a favour.' He paused. 'I wondered. . .I wondered if you would come to the charity ball as my partner? That's if your friend hasn't a prior claim.'

'My friend?'

'Didn't you say he's called Tom?'

'Why on earth should I be going to the ball with Tom? As far as I'm aware he doesn't know anything about it. I'd be thrilled to be your partner.' A sudden thought struck her. 'Oh, aren't you taking Fiona?'

Neil looked at her, shame faced. 'I don't really want to go with Fiona, or at least to be considered as her escort. She'll have me running the charity auction, greeting people when they arrive. . . Oh, I don't know. I'd rather be an anonymous figure, just there for the enjoyment. Selfish, perhaps, but. . .' He took hold of the points of her collar and pulled her close. 'So, sweet Sally, dear Sally, would you save me from Fiona's clutches?'

For the second time that morning, disappointment almost overwhelmed her.

'So it's not that you want me, it's that you don't want Fiona?' She swallowed hard. '"Wholesome Sally" to the rescue. Will I get paid for the evening? Is it to be counted as part of my job?'

Hastily, Neil stood back. 'You have a very nasty tongue at times, haven't you? If you don't want to come with me, say so.' He turned and pushed open the door of his room. 'Don't put yourself out, just let me know when you've decided,' he called over his shoulder. As he disappeared inside a ray of sun briefly highlighted the dark gloss of his hair.

'Damn!' Furiously Sally kicked the wall, then swore again as her foot hit the wooden edge of the skirting-board. Hopping dramatically, she rubbed her toe, its sharp pain distracting her for a moment. But as she limped back to the reception desk and perched on her chair the ache in her heart far outweighed that of her bruised foot.

Why couldn't he have asked me for myself? she thought. Why does there have to be a reason other than wanting my company? Angrily she seized a couple of files and pushed them to one side. 'I've a good mind to let him stew, to leave him to Fiona's tender mercies,' she said aloud. But she knew she wouldn't do that. The thought of Neil spending an evening with Fiona was too awful to contemplate. However her invitation had come about, Sally knew she couldn't forgo an opportunity of being with him. 'That's if the invite still stands,' she muttered aloud. 'You could have blown it, Sally Chalmers.'

'Talking to yourself? First signs, they say.'

'What do you want, Tom?' Impatiently Sally looked up as Tom came in and leant on the desk. 'I'm at work, in case you hadn't noticed, and I shouldn't be gossiping with you.' Ostentatiously, she opened one of the patient's files and studied it.

'I've not come to gossip. Though I see you have one patient of interest.' He smiled at Sally's gasp of horror. 'Yes, that's right, a certain soap star.'

'How did you know. . .?' she began.

But Tom hadn't time to answer. 'My God, who's that?'

Sally had no need to see whose were the high-heeled shoes clicking across the hall. The musky perfume told her even before she saw Fiona.

'Neil back?' The other woman barely paused before setting off along the corridor.

'Just a second, I'll see if he's free. He. . .'

'No need to ask him; I'm sure he'll see me.'

'She's not a patient, surely?' Tom whistled softly through his teeth, watching Fiona's sway of the hips as she disappeared from view.

'Tom, stop drooling. That's an old friend of Neil's. I want to ask you, how did you know about Melody?'

'Went looking for a coffee and happened to see her. Why, is it a problem?'

'You won't say anything, will you?'

'Course not. What do you think I am?'

'I'm not sure,' Sally muttered anxiously. But her annoyance at Fiona's off-hand manner and the arrogant set of her shoulders dragged her thoughts away from Tom. If Neil wanted her to go to the ball as his partner, she would. And she would make sure that she had something absolutely stunning to wear that would knock everyone's eyes out. Just let Miss Slingsby ignore her then.

'Melody get away OK?' Sally glanced up at the sound of Neil's voice.

'Yes. She was terribly excited and will probably drive her parents daft, but she was fine.'

'Right, I've Mr Whitton to do this afternoon. He's coming as an outpatient, so there isn't any reason for you to hang about once he's arrived and is in Theatre. Unless. . .' he raised an enquiring eyebrow '. . .unless you'd like to see the operation?'

'I'd love to. I've nothing in particular planned for later.' Neatly she flipped the duvet with its clean cover on to Melody's bed, bundled the dirty linen in her arms and went towards the door. 'And I'd very much like to go to the ball as your partner,' she added, hurrying to the laundry-room before Neil had a chance to reply.

'Whew!' she gasped to herself, pressing the sheets into a linen bag and tying the tape firmly. 'I hope I haven't committed myself to something I can't cope with.'

Humming softly under her breath, she hurried to the reception area and poked her head around the office door.

'What time is Mr Whitton getting here, Trish?'

'Should be arriving shortly.' Trish glanced at the miniature clock on her desk. 'I think he's booked for five p.m., straight after work.'

Sally pulled a face. 'Makes it a long day for Neil, doesn't it?'

'Don't worry about him. He's tough.' Trish glanced over her glasses before returning to the word processor.

'"Don't worry about him". How can I avoid it?' Sally muttered as she went back to Reception and sorted the charts for the new admissions into their relevant dates. 'I can't stop myself.'

Must be love, an inner voice muttered inside her head.

'But it can't be,' Sally whispered, quickly smothering the thought. 'It's just that I'm susceptible to a bit of attention, after Tom.' But she knew that her brave words weren't true, and when Neil rang later to ask if she was coming to watch Mr Whitton's surgery she was thankful that a mask would be hiding her expression from Neil's searching gaze.

He took her arm as she hurried into the anaesthetic-room after changing, and for one mad moment she wondered if he had guessed how she felt.

'Just to warn you,' he murmured, 'that when a patient has a local anaesthetic I don't mention instruments, incisions, anything to do with the surgery. OK? No sudden noises, either.' His eyes were warm above his mask, and despite her earlier resolve to be nothing but professional her yearning was so strong that she thought he must sense it.

But he went into Theatre to sit beside the operating-table, and her personal worries were pushed to one side as she watched the operation.

What a waste of talent, Sally thought, just to help someone's vanity. She watched carefully as Neil injected the local anaesthetic. Why isn't he using that amazing skill to operate on babies, for example, instead of for profit? But she knew there was no answer, at least not one that would satisfy her.

All the instruments were minute, the scalpel scarcely visible as Neil made tiny cuts in John Whitton's upper lids then just below the lashes of the lower ones.

Despite her interest, she couldn't prevent a small

shiver as Neil pushed out the fatty pads around the eyes and trimmed excess skin, finally suturing with diminutive stitches.

It seemed strange to Sally that the only conversation was on general topics, no one mentioning the procedure except when Neil's dark brown voice explained it to Mr Whitton; she noticed that even the instrument bowl was lined with a towel so that the patient wouldn't hear any noise.

'Now, just rest in the clinic for an hour,' Neil instructed as he eventually peeled away the towels and helped John Whitton to sit up. 'Is your wife coming to fetch you?'

The patient nodded blearily, obviously still under the effects of his sedation.

'Good. Then when you get home, straight to bed. Take it easy for the next couple of days, no bending or stretching or lifting heavy weights, and then we'll have you back to remove the stitches.' Muttering a brief 'thank you', Neil hurried from the theatre as the porter arrived with a wheelchair, and by the time Sally had changed back into her ordinary uniform there was no sign of the surgeon.

'Well, thanks for the lecture on the op,' she muttered, disappointed that he had gone without a word. 'Though perhaps it's just as well,' she told her reflection in the changing-room mirror, surprised that her self-awareness about her feelings had not altered her appearance. Their intensity should emblazon them across her forehead in fluorescent colours. But the possibility of Neil's horror or, even worse, pity, if he did discover how she felt was enough to push such thoughts aside, and she consciously straightened her back as she went out of the front door and climbed into her car.

CHAPTER EIGHT

GIDDY with fatigue, Sally picked up her suitcase from the carousel and waited patiently for Neil and Mike to collect the remaining luggage. They stacked all the equipment, and a mound of bags and boxes, on to trolleys, ready for transfer to the small aircraft waiting on the tarmac outside. Swirls of fog outside the large plate-glass windows obscured any view of the Brazilian city of Belém, tendrils hanging in the air like the lowering cloud they had just come through on landing.

'Can you take that black case for me, Sally, the one with my name in the corner?' Neil's voice jerked her into wakefulness. 'Don't lose sight of it, will you? It has all my drugs in it.'

Wearily Sally plodded in the two men's footsteps, with an envious glance at Hilary, who looked as alert as ever despite their recent ten-hour flight from Heathrow.

'Why can't all the equipment be transferred directly from one plane to the other?' Sally grumbled. 'Save all this bother.'

'We can't risk any of our stuff going astray; Neil always checks everything himself, particularly if we're changing from a scheduled flight to a local one. Not that the airport staff aren't capable, but if anything's missing it's not like losing your make-up when you go on holiday. We can't replace instruments or medicines, especially in some of the out-of-the-way places we get called to.' Hilary stared sympathetically. 'You look tired.'

'I am. As well as being jet-lagged, I'm still stunned by the discovery of Neil's other life. I thought he was at a conference when he disappeared from the clinic.'

'That's what he intends people to think. He doesn't like to make a big issue of the fact that he uses some of the profits from the clinic to pay for expeditions such as this one.'

'Nothing like hiding your light under a bushel. Why does he want to keep it a secret?'

'He's not one to boast about his good deeds.' Hilary laughed softly. 'Pretends to be the hard-headed businessman, but underneath he's a big softy.'

Sally blinked at the description. Neil, a big softy! It wasn't the word she would use to describe him, though he was always very caring in his approach to his clinic patients. But she had assumed that that was partly due to it being good business sense. Perhaps she had misjudged him. 'How far is this island?' she yawned.

'Setuba is about three hours' flying time.'

'And do all our patients have cleft lips and palates?'

'Just about. Because it's an island, there is a lot of inbreeding, so a family tendency towards lips and palates occurs much more frequently. Unfortunately, quite a lot are adults, and getting back clear speech isn't likely. But I believe we have several children to operate on, and they should do very well.'

'What about post-op care?'

'Very straightforward. Stitches out of lips in about four days, and we leave plenty of hydrogen peroxide for cleaning. Palate repairs just have to rinse their mouths thoroughly after food, normally no problem. Surprisingly enough, there is usually little in the way of post-operative infection.'

'That's amazing, without any follow-up clinics.'

Hilary paused as they reached the departure gate and pulled out passports to show to the official.

'Sometimes we go through without any formalities; at other times everything has to be checked and double-checked.'

'Including the luggage?' Sally's thoughts moved sluggishly; everything seemed so different from when she had flown on holiday.

'Again, Neil tries to keep as much of the gear under his eye as he can. We went through the scanner in the transit lounge.'

'Not that we're likely to be carrying explosives,' Sally giggled feebly. 'As we're the only ones on the plane.'

The cases were stacked on the ground by the aircraft. Two pilots, Hollywood-smart in white uniforms with navy flashes on their shoulders, sketched a salute as Neil's party arrived. The mist was clearing rapidly, early morning sunshine piercing the vapour and bringing a heavy warmth to the air.

'The luggage has to be loaded before we go aboard. I'll check each case, then we can get ourselves comfortable.' Neil smiled reassuringly at Sally before disappearing up the flight of four steps into the body of the plane.

'We look after ourselves during the trip,' Hilary muttered. 'No welcoming air steward, but there should be sandwiches and coffee available.'

'All I want to do is sleep.' Sally yawned again, wrinkling her nose against the sharp smell of aircraft fuel. Restlessly she shifted from one foot to the other while their precious cargo was stacked, before following the rest of the medical team inside.

'Gosh, it's small, isn't it?'

Astonished, she stared at the two rows of leather-covered seats, the roof of the plane preventing any but the shortest person from standing upright.

'This is quite roomy compared with some,' Neil laughed as he beckoned Sally to a window-seat and slid into place beside her.

Hilary and Mike settled at the rear, the pilot pulled up the steps, locked the door and turned to face them.

'In case of emergency,' he said in barely accented English, with just an attractive softness about the sibilants. 'The exits are here and here. If there is need, oxygen masks come from these ceiling-points as in larger planes. . .' His voice continued with the short safety lecture but Sally was peering from the window, amazed at how near the ground they were as the engines fired into life and the seatbelt lights flashed up on the overhead strip.

'Your first flight in a small plane?' Neil's voice was sympathetic as Sally nodded, chewing busily at a peppermint. Even though she had cleaned her teeth at the airport, she still had a terrible taste in her mouth. Probably a bit like poor Melody, she thought, wondering for a moment how the young actress was coping now she was at home.

But she had no more time to worry about things in the UK, for the engines surged into sudden life, there

was a crackle of voices from the radios, then the little
aircraft hurtled along the bumpy tarmac and was air-
borne before Sally had time to catch her breath.

The gradual lightening of the sky was enough to
pierce the fog for a moment, and she caught a glimpse
of streets and houses below, and what looked like a
shanty town of cardboard and corrugated metal before
the plane swept into cloud-cover and soared into blazing sunshine above.

'What a short take-off.' She smiled at Neil as he
stretched his legs into the gangway before she stared
once more from the window.

It was still difficult to believe the she was actually
travelling with Neil's group, *en route* to a small island
near the South American coast.

When Neil had asked if she had a current passport,
bewildered, she'd wondered if he was going to suggest
a holiday! But, no. He was off to do reconstructive
surgery on the indigenous population of Setuba, and
wanted her to go along.

Sally glanced at the others. Hilary was already doz-
ing, her head rolling against the back of the seat, her
mouth slightly open. Mike had a large medical textbook on his lap, but gazed with unseeing eyes towards
the front of the plane. Neil, beside her, studied papers
from his briefcase.

They were all so relaxed, but then Hilary and Mike
had known about Neil's other life from the start.
Despite her excitement at being asked to come, Sally
still had mixed feelings that Neil hadn't trusted her
from the word go.

'I'm sorry I didn't tell you before about these

expeditions.' Neil's dark brown voice echoed her thoughts so exactly that she wondered for a moment if she had spoken them aloud.

'It's something I've never discussed with staff—except for Hilary, Mike and Trish, of course—because if it became public knowledge all the wrong aspects would be exaggerated.' He shrugged. 'And I prefer to keep the clinic and this side of my life separate.'

'What started you on these trips?'

'I spent a short time in West Africa—volunteers abroad, type of thing—and obviously there was no plastic surgery available. I did several sessions there and, when I got back to the UK, kept in touch with the volunteer organisation. They let me know of places where I can be useful, and that's how it came about.'

'And when did you decide you could trust me not to spill the beans?' Sally's voice was cold.

'I think I knew right from the start that you would be discreet. After all, discretion is a big part of our job. Famous clients—not that I get many of those—might not want the whole world to know about their latest face-lift. And Melody certainly wouldn't have wanted press pictures of her poor little smashed face.' He was silent, gazing thoughtfully along the narrow gangway, then turned to her again. 'I had to be sure. You realize that, don't you? Have I upset you?'

Sally shrugged.

'Well, I apologise, but I can't risk any slip-up. The fewer people in on a secret, the less the risk of discovery, and I don't want any client to know about these visits.' He leaned close and spoke softly. 'Am I forgiven?'

'Nothing to forgive,' she said shortly. 'You don't owe me anything.'

She stared at a view of coastline and rough seas just visible through patches of cloud. Why on earth had Neil been doubtful about trusting her with his secret? He should have known instinctively that she would do anything rather then cause him harm of any sort.

Perhaps she was being unduly sensitive. If it was something he had been used to keeping to himself, it would be difficult to break the habit, however he might feel towards her.

'What made you ask me? After all, I don't fool myself that I have any professional expertise to offer.'

He studied her hard and long, without speaking, his eyes darkened almost to purple, his expression enigmatic. 'Some time I'll tell you, but I had a very good reason, I promise.'

God, I wish I didn't blush so easily, Sally thought, at the betraying warmth she felt touch her cheeks. There was something about the way he looked at her. . .

But she had no chance to dwell on Neil's words for Mike was at the front of the plane, dispensing coffees all round from a small water-boiler set in a cupboard, noisily squirting steam.

Sally sniffed appreciatively as Neil passed hers across.

'Feeling any less tired?' Vigorously he stirred sugar into his cup.

'I think so. I've never flown for such a long time at one stretch, and stretch is all I want to do right now.

An hour's aerobics or a brisk jog seem the most attractive things I can think of.'

'Well, there aren't any aerobics classes where we're going, but there is a beautiful ocean, and we have one day to unwind and get our breath back before the real work begins. Perhaps a swim will be a good substitute.'

He sipped thoughtfully, his eyes fixed straight ahead.

'What is the procedure when we arrive?'

'Hilary will fill you in; I have to talk to Mike for a bit.'

Neil and Hilary changed seats, moving awkwardly in the narrow aisle, and Sally felt somehow bereft without Neil's comforting presence at her side. She sighed as she turned to Hilary.

'What do you want to know?' The theatre sister dug into her bag and produced a packet of boiled sweets, offering one to Sally.

'Thanks. I want to know everything. I feel completely lost,' Sally muttered anxiously as she popped the sweet into her mouth.

'First day there, we rest,' Hilary began. 'Get over our jet-lag. It can't be counted as time wasted because we wouldn't be very efficient if we tried to start work immediately. Usually we check out the facilities, if there are any, then make good any deficit in anaesthetics, drugs, that sort of thing. On this island there is a small hospital of sorts, run by nuns, so at least everything should be clean. Sometimes we have to wash all the floors and walls before we start.'

'Must be a challenge.' Sally frowned. 'Doesn't all that responsibility make you nervous?'

Hilary shook her head. 'I love it—back to grass

roots, so to speak. After all the luxury at home, with every facility to hand, it's so different—enjoyable, though. Trying to adapt and make do is very good for all of us. Of course, Neil brings all his instruments; there would be no way we could manage without those.'

'Mike's the one who has to make the greatest adjustment,' Neil added from behind them. 'You wait till you see how limited the anaesthetics are. If we have piped oxygen, we're lucky.'

'And all the cases here will have cleft lips or palates repaired, is that right?' Sally looked over her shoulder, her face only inches from Neil's. She tried hard to concentrate on what he was saying, but all the time she was conscious of everything about him: his half-smile, his penetrating gaze, his clean fresh scent.

'Because of family tendencies and inbreeding it means that a lot of the locals have the same problem,' he explained, apparently unaware of the reason for her absorption in his every word. 'Ideally, of course, we would like to do speech therapy, expecially for the older patients, but. . .' He shrugged eloquently.

'What language do they speak on the island?'

'A mixture of Portuguese and an Indian dialect. Difficult to understand, even without palate defects.'

Sally turned to face the front, anticipation lifting her earlier nervousness. From what she had been told so far, she couldn't see exactly what her role would be. But she fully intended to enjoy every moment, the bonus of being in Neil's company an extra pleasure to be savoured over the next few days.

Smiling, she drifted into a doze, the soft drone of

the engine a lullaby difficult to resist. Her dreams of
Neil had him holding a large scalpel, which he used
to slash open a coconut shell. He was on one knee,
ceremoniously offering her a drink from it, when she
felt a gentle shake.

'Sally, Sally, wake up, We're coming in to land.'
Rubbing her eyes, she pulled herself upright, and
realised that while she had slept Neil had returned to
the seat beside her; what she had assumed to be a
pillow was, in fact, his cotton-clad shoulder. Hastily
she looked out of the window. Below was an enormous
estuary that stretched for miles, the swirling water
frothing like cappuccino coffee as it reached the edge
of the waves.

She could just see the island, like an elongated tri-
angle, the wider end towards the tumbling river-mouth.

'Nearly there,' Neil said softly, leaning across her to
look at the rapidly approaching land. 'We're not far
from the equator, so you'll have to be very careful
about sunburn. Especially as there's a continuous
easterly breeze, which gives a false idea of the temperature.'

'Have you been here before?' Sally stared at him
curiously.

'No, but one thing I've learnt in these trips is to do
my homework and make sure I know as much as I can
about the place before we get there. Then, if we're
reasonably well-prepared, we can deal with things on
the spot.'

The plane began a rapid descent, the greenery that
covered the centre of the island looking more and more
luxuriant as they came in to land. Surf creamed the

edge of the shoreline like lace, defining the soft white sand.

'Looks like Robinson Crusoe's island,' Sally remarked nervously. Now that they were nearly there, her anticipation was lost in a surge of panic. Chewing quickly on her peppermint, she stared at the small airfield, a white-painted building sitting neatly at the edge of the uneven tarmac that jarred the plane as it touched down.

'This way.' An official strode ahead of them, clutching his clipboard in front of him, his sleek dark hair undisturbed by the breeze that, as far as Sally was concerned, brought a welcome relief from the overwhelming heat of the morning.

'What now?' She had to skip slightly to keep up. Where was the slow languorous pace she had pictured in the tropics? She hurried along beside Neil, her bag clutched in one hand, her other smoothing desperately at her hair as it flew in a cloud about her face.

'Once airport formalities are completed there's about an hour's drive to the hospital. Then we rest for twenty-four hours before we hold our first clinic.'

'Do you have any idea how many patients there will be?'

But Neil didn't have time to answer for they had arrived at a Customs shed, their precious baggage already on trolleys, two smiling, dark-faced porters in grey shirts and trousers ready to escort them to a waiting Range Rover.

The driver swiftly loaded the gear aboard and Sally, helped up by a tug on her elbow, clambered into the seat beside Hilary. She longed for a shower; her cotton slacks were crumpled and her T-shirt clung to her back.

Thrown from side to side as they bumped over rutted roads, she barely had time to notice as the sun cast its shadows through the fringe of palm trees, an occasional flash of brilliant colour just visible when noisy parakeets flew from branch to branch. It was surprisingly dusty, despite the humidity, and small eddies of brown earth trailed their progress.

Before long they came to a square, surrounded by pink-washed buildings, the curved roofs and decorated fronts very reminiscent of houses that Sally had once seen during a holiday in Portugal.

Black-feathered chickens pecked busily in the roadside dust as the Range Rover drove through a gate set in a wall on which the broken patches of plaster resembled some fungal growth.

But inside there was a pleasant garden, though overgrown with lush greenery and bright splashes of blue, purple and red from exotic, fleshy blooms. The splashing sounds of a fountain in the centre of the courtyard seemed to cool the overheated air.

Almost before the vehicle had pulled up outside a heavy oak door it was flung back, and a white-robed nun, her face creased in welcome, the fine lines of her skin radiating from her smiling eyes, hurried towards them.

'Welcome.' Sally blinked, startled at the strong Irish lilt in the woman's voice but by this time everything seemed unreal and, after a moment's pause, it wasn't strange to be on an island to the north of Brazil and hear soft tones that would have been more at home in Waterford or Donegal.

'I'm Sister Antonia.' Lifting the hem of her skirt, she came to the side of the vehicle, and Sally could see that whatever else in her appearance might have been dried by the tropical sun the eyes were still a deep, Irish blue, with astonishingly black lashes, making her look like a surprised tortoiseshell cat.

'This way, this way. I expect you could do with something to eat and drink, then will want your beds as soon as possible, no doubt.'

Sally, following the others, nodded heartfelt agreement. She seemed to be the only one who was nearly asleep on her feet.

'Coffee, bread and honey, some eggs.' Like a society hostess, Sister Antonia gestured towards a table in the simply furnished kitchen, its wooden floor and highly polished furniture gleaming. It was remarkably peaceful, no sounds penetrating from outside, just the noise of a kettle singing on a woodburning stove in the corner.

Apart from the sister, who started to pull out chairs around the table, they could have been the only inhabitants.

After a quick visit to a small washroom where, despite the rusty water that spluttered fitfully from the tap, Sally felt refreshed by her wash, the four of them sat down, appreciative of the frugal meal set out on the table.

'I'm too tired to eat,' Sally murmured, thirstily downing her third cup of coffee.

'You eat whenever you can,' Neil said sternly. 'The next couple of days are going to be hectic, and we need to eat and drink properly to keep ourselves at maximum efficiency.'

'Yes, sir!' Sally answered crisply, obeying instructions. Despite her doubts it was no hardship, for the bread was delicious, newly baked with a thick crust and she surprised herself by managing to clear her plate of eggs, following them with more of the bread and some honey.

'I'll get someone to show you to your rooms.' Hovering in the background as they finally drained the last of the coffee, Sister Antonia pointed to an opening which led into the centre garden and then to a half-roofed walkway, with doors along one side, partly covered by trailing bougainvillaea.

'I shall be fine here, thank you.' Carefully Sally set her bag down on the uncarpeted wooden floor of her room, starkly furnished, but with an inviting bed in the corner, its white woven coverlet a contrast to the dark mahogany of the wooden frame. Apart from a small rail with hooks and a chair at the bedside the room was bare, but pleasantly cool air brought a drift of flowery scents through the screened window, which kept out the light of the blazing sun. In a picture above the bed the vivid blue dress of a robust Madonna was the only colour in the room.

Too tired even to clean her teeth, Sally rinsed her mouth with some of the bottled water at the bedside, stripped off her clothes, and tumbled naked beneath the coarsely woven cotton sheet. And the lullaby sounds of the fountain outside, a whisper of voices from afar, and the sound of sandalled feet as someone walked along the passage outside, were enough to send her into a deep and restful sleep.

CHAPTER NINE

'WHAT do you want me to do?' Bewildered, and feeling
very much in the way, Sally stared at the whirl of
activity, wondering again why Neil had asked her to
be part of the team. It was still early morning, barely
five o'clock, and the sky had only just begun to lighten
from its night-time indigo, but inside the small, tiled
clinic-room Neil, Hilary and Mike had gone into action
like some well-drilled army squad.

Hilary, just outside the door, laid out paper-wrapped
packs neatly in line on an iron-framed bedstead, for
there were no spare trolleys; Mike was checking two
cylinders—one black for oxygen, one blue for nitrous
oxide—on an old-fashioned anaesthetic machine
and Neil counted artery forceps, setting ten to a clip
before placing them in a small steriliser filled with
boiling water.

'You can give me a hand,' Hilary called. 'Don't
worry about not pulling your weight,' the Theatre sister
assured her as Sally hurried to her side. 'Once the
patients start arriving, you'll have plenty to do. In the
meantime, you can put these packs in order. I'd like
gowns and gloves here, keyhole towels here—they're
the ones we place around the operation site—then
ordinary towels on the right. All the packs are labelled,
should be straightforward.' She pushed the cardboard
box containing the packs nearer Sally with her knee,

and went back to the operating-area.

Happily Sally set to. She still felt disorientated. She had woken early, when the sky was still an inky well of blackness lit only by diamond-bright stars, their brilliance undiluted by any street-lamps.

As she'd gazed from her window at the tropical night she had asked herself why Neil had asked her to come. It was difficult to understand for, eager though she was to help, and thrilled to be included, there must be others more qualified than she was in such a setting. Now, looking at the bustle around her, her doubts returned with greater force.

She glanced through the open doorway to where Neil was working. Moving with his usual economical grace, he went from job to job. He must have felt her gaze, and gave her an almighty wink, his grin lighting up his face.

'All right, Sally?'

Her breath caught in her throat as she smiled back, almost overwhelmed by the strength of her emotions. Working automatically, the sections of packs growing all the time, her mind was free to drift, to wonder what would happen when they went back to the UK.

Had she betrayed her feelings for Neil, and was that why she had been asked to come, because he felt sorry for her? A sort of consolation prize, perhaps, as he wasn't prepared to give himself? The thought made her shiver. If he wasn't interested in her she couldn't see herself continuing to work at Kynaston in the future, though how she would find the courage to put him out of her life, she didn't know. But cut her losses she would, if it was necessary.

'How are you doing?' he called softly, interrupting her tangled thoughts.

Hilary pushed her fair hair back from her face as she returned, not giving Sally time to reply. 'Nearly ready this end. Well done, Sally, that's great. I think we already have a queue, so I'm going to scrub. Would you put that trolley on the far side for me, please, and get a pack of sterile gowns handy?' She went to the sink, standing beside Neil, who already had his hands under running water.

'How do you manage about assessing what the patients need? After all, you've no idea of their previous health—if they're anaemic, have high blood pressure, heart problems that would need extra care.' Moving behind Hilary, Sally swiftly tied the tapes of her sterile gown, then held open a pack of rubber gloves and counted swabs as Hilary checked them on the instrument trolley.

'Mike and I examine each patient briefly.' Neil had moved with his back to her, waiting, like Hilary, for Sally to tie the tapes of his gown. 'We've got certain parameters to guide us as to whether someone is OK for surgery. I suppose it must be experience, but it seems to work. Anyway——' he raised his eyebrows above his mask '——no looking for problems. We've got a theatre to run.

'We're lucky here,' he continued. 'We've actually got an operating-table, of sorts, and an overhead light. Sometimes on these trips we don't even have that much.'

He and Hilary stood side by side, their gloved hands folded in front of them, no sign of nervousness from either surgeon or Theatre sister.

'Patient number one is on the way.' Mike's head appeared briefly through the door, his Theatre cap pushed askew, his glasses misted in the steadily rising temperature.

Already beads of perspiration had settled on Sally's forehead, and the length of her spine felt damp. Goodness knew what it would be like later in the day. But she didn't have time to worry about being hot, for Mike had arrived with the first patient, and from then on it was a production line of surgery that soon became a blur of mixed impressions.

No time to watch the actual surgery. She was aware only of blood-soaked swabs, the clink of instruments in the bowl, Neil's murmured requests, children whimpering in the ante-room, the squeak of wheels, mopping Neil's forehead, and the open window, their only form of air-conditioning, through which drifted an unexpected spicy scent from the flowers outside in sharp contrast to the smell of ether and antiseptic.

'Sally, can you get me one of those packs in the corner, please?' Hilary pointed across the room.

Her feet slipping in her Theatre clogs, her hair clinging to her scalp, Sally hurried to fetch the pack. She wasn't sure if this was the fourth or fifth operation, she had lost count, but she knew that she was flagging and would have to rest soon.

Neil and Mike didn't even look particularly tired, blast 'em, she thought as she helped to lift the unconscious child on to the table, wincing at the sight of the grossly deformed upper lip.

She paused to stare, fascinated, as Neil swabbed the

lip, then draped a towel across, shielding all but the operating-site.

'Ready, Mike?'

The anaesthetist nodded in answer, picking up a syringe and injecting a little more sedative into a vein.

'Just oxygen and nitrous oxide—enough to keep the patients under—and everything else is given intra-venously,' Mike explained, in answer to Sally's questioning look.

With a tiny mapping-pen and blue dye, Neil drew zig-zag lines on each side of the lip's division. Then he cut the lines with a sharply pointed scalpel, dabbing at the small arteries that bloomed like tiny red flowers on the skin.

Trimming excess tissue from each side, he gradually pulled the zig-zag cuts into line, holding the points in place with small hooks.

'Luckily this lip isn't too badly distorted. We try as much as possible to make a normal cupid's bow along the top and a natural dimple, if we can.' He pointed with the end of the forceps.

'This lip isn't too badly distorted?' Sally gaped in disbelief.

'If there is a double cleft it's much worse. Then the surgery can be tricky, for it means there is virtually no upper lip at all.'

Neatly he stitched, with fine nylon thread, and Hilary snipped the suture ends as he quickly knotted them in place.

Impressed, Sally studied his work. Even with the slight swelling that had already developed, the lip looked almost normal.

'That's marvellous,' she muttered admiringly.

'Not marvellous, but a pretty good job. Right, into the recovery-room, if you can call it that,' he laughed.

'Who's taking care of them outside?' Sally suddenly realised that she had been so busy she'd given no thought to the patients once they had gone from Theatre.

'Two of the nuns who've had some nursing experience are supervising, otherwise relatives help with the care.' He gestured towards Mike. 'With the genius of my colleague there, it's usually only a very short time before they wake up.'

As if the little boy had heard, while Hilary dabbed the suture line dry, removed towels and put them to one side he gave a sleepy cry, and stirred on the table.

'Right on cue, Mike,' Neil laughed approvingly. Cardboard splints applied to his arms, to prevent any scratching, their patient was wheeled from the theatre. There was just time to swab the floor and worktops with carbolic and then the next patient, probably in her teens, was brought in.

One after another, the cases followed. Two older people had cleft palates. With these, Neil lifted part of the lining of the upper mouth, cutting round it with a scalpel, then pulled the two flaps into line, like closing wings, before suturing.

Sally felt as though life was nothing but green gowns which she tied, whiffs of gas from the anaesthetic machine, wheeling another patient into Theatre, wheeling him outside when finished.

They had a break during the middle of the day, pausing for drinks and a cold meat sandwich and a rest, though Sally barely tasted her food. It was just fuel to keep her going.

Starting again at four o'clock, the day followed its earlier pattern. When they had first begun to operate Sally's mind had buzzed with questions. How did they prevent infection? Who did the nursing? Who would remove the stitches? But as the day wore on everything was concentrated into a sharp focus of aching back, tired legs, and perspiration so profuse that she couldn't understand why they didn't all suffer heatstroke.

It was galling to see that the other three didn't appear too uncomfortable. Apart from a darkening of his hairline, Neil looked as fresh when they eventually finished the last case of the day as when they had started that morning.

But his sigh as he pulled off his cap and gloves seemed to reach from the depths of his rubber boots. Sluggishly they moved as one to a small sitting-room where a young, dark-skinned girl was pouring coffee and glasses of iced mango juice.

Sally swallowed hers even before sinking on to a wooden chair.

'Sit here.' Neil pulled forward the only comfortable seat in the room.

'If I relax at all, I shall fall asleep,' Sally groaned. She ran her fingers through her hair, grimacing at the clumps of sweat-soaked strands. 'I'm exhausted. I don't know how you can keep on operating as you do. All of you.' She swung round to face the others.

'If you think that's a long day, I must arrange for you to see some microsurgery when we get back. Anything up to sixteen hours for a single operation.

And everything viewed through a magnifier.'

'Don't.' Sally groaned again, stretching her arms above her head. 'I had pictured a stroll along the beach before retiring, but I'm too tired to do anything except shower and lay down my weary head.'

'That's a shame.' A disappointed frown crossed Neil's face. 'I'd hoped to go for a swim before turning in.'

'No can do. Ask Mike or Hilary.'

'You've been a great help.' Gently Neil took her hand as she went past. 'See you in the morning.' He pulled her close and lightly kissed her on the cheek.

'Don't, I'm all sweaty.'

'Tastes pretty good to me,' he said softly. With his face only inches from hers, Sally could see everything in sharp focus. His eyes looked almost blue, with tiny flecks of gold reflected from the harsh overhead light, his skin olive, his teeth a flash of white. 'God, you do look tired. I'd better not get any closer, with this sandpaper skin.' He grinned as he dragged his hand across his chin, the rasp against his emergent beard audible in the silence of the room.

'I. . .'

'Right, you two, stop canoodling, we've got a theatre to prepare for tomorrow.' Hilary's voice cut in sharply. 'I've cleaned all the instruments, put out towels to be washed, filled the small theatre steriliser and set out more rubber gloves for the morning. We only have to. . .'

'Not Sally,' Neil said firmly, putting an arm around her. 'She's too tired.'

'I'm certainly not too tired to do my share.' Indignantly Sally hurried back to the operating-room.

Aren't I contrary? she thought, grinning to herself as she tidied the table used for instruments. I hate my wholesome image, long to be treated delicately, but when Neil is considerate I take offence. Busily she washed the operating-area and, under Hilary's directions, set the sterile packs in order, ready for the following day.

At last everything was tidy. 'Is that it?' Sally slumped on to a stool.

'Yes, all set. Do you think you'll last the pace?' Hilary asked quietly.

'Anything anyone else can do, I can manage as well. But——' wearily Sally rubbed the middle of her back '—I shan't be sorry to get to bed. I don't think I could have gone on much longer.'

Footsteps dragging, Sally looked in the small annexe as she passed, but it was empty. Too tired to worry that she hadn't said goodnight, she set off along the corridor.

And she was able to summon a last burst of energy for her shower before tumbling into bed, where she fell immediately into a deep and dreamless sleep.

Sally sat back in her canvas chair and sighed, utter contentment warming her.

'That fish was delicious.' The four of them had just finished eating, the first proper sit-down meal they had really managed to enjoy since their arrival. It was the evening of the fourth day, and tomorrow would mark their return to the UK.

Sally couldn't believe how the time had not merely

flown, but rocketed past. Each day had followed a similar pattern—a five o'clock start before the day's heat had really taken hold, a day of non-stop work in the operating-room, and a quick review of the patients of the previous day, Neil frantically scribbling notes or dictating them into his mini-cassette in that dark, handsome voice.

She still found it difficult to believe how little follow-up care the patients—a mixture of South American Indian and Portuguese—needed. Their stoicism was a revelation—none complaining after surgery, all making an effort to speak as Neil went round the make-shift ward last thing. He, too, was a revelation—the smooth, elegant figure of home transformed into a frontiersman in khaki shirt and shorts, moving quietly in his soft boots, doing far more than his share of the chores.

'We all muck in and help with the clearing up,' Hilary had explained. 'With only basic requirements available, every precious item, drug, piece of equipment, what have you, has to be accounted for. That's why *you've* had to wash down the operating-area with carbolic at the end of the shift,' the Theatre sister had continued, 'rather than getting someone local to do it.'

Sally pushed her plate to one side. 'We've been very lucky to have Sister Antonia here, haven't we?'

'In what way?' Neil looked intently at her.

'Well, with her knowledge of the local language and nursing training.'

'True, she's been a marvellous help. And you have as well.'

Sally glowed at the compliment. 'I hope so. I'd hate

to think I'd come along just for the ride.' She chewed thoughtfully at a slice of mango. 'In some ways, I'll be sorry to leave,' she surprised herself by saying.

An oil lamp lit the table, heavy-winged moths crashing against it at intervals. Shrill noises, which she had discovered were made by small tree frogs, piped a background chorus. The glasses of wine, the slices of mango with juice spilling out of them, the intermittent conversation, all combined to bring a sense of unreality to the scene, and Sally wouldn't have been at all surprised to have woken and found it all a dream.

But it was no dream. She was actually sitting beside Neil on a tropical island, and every so often he looked at her in the lamplight, his hair brushed back after his shower, his white shirt and shorts emphasising his tanned skin and the outline of his lean powerful body.

'I'm for a late night swim.' Without warning, he stood, stretching his arms above his head. 'I feel as though I've been crouched forward over an operating-table for years, not days. Anyone else care to join me?'

'Not for me.' Hilary shuddered. 'You never know what sea creature might be waiting to pounce in the dark.'

'Nor me. Mike shook his head. 'I'm going to sit here, watch the moonlight, and steadily sip my wine until it's time for bed.'

'Sally? Don't you let me down as well,' he begged, holding out his arms towards her.

'I don't mind. Where are you going for your swim?'

'The beach is only a short walk away. Get your swimsuit; I'll see you in a few minutes.'

Swiftly she hurried into the dimly lit building to her

room, slipped on a plain navy swimsuit and picked up a towel and multi-coloured cotton wrap.

'Are there really any creatures?' Moving close, Sally took Neil's arm as they crossed the pot-holed road towards the beach. The sea could be heard above the noise of the chattering of the villagers, a gentle swooshing sound that grew louder as they moved on to the sand.

'There's nothing more dangerous than the odd crab who might be disturbed by us. Not cold, are you?' He draped his towel over his shoulder, and put an arm around her.

'No, I'm fine.' She looked at a picture postcard view, the moon more gold than silver, painting a pathway across the murmuring waves. Sugar-fine sand filled their footprints as soon as they moved, obliterating all trace of them.

'I'm not too sure about the swim now,' Sally muttered nervously. 'The sea looks awfully black.'

'Come on, we won't go in too deep if you'd rather not. Just a few splashes at the water's edge.' Not giving her time to draw back, Neil seized her hand and ran towards the water. It was warm, like silk caressing her legs, streams of phosphoresence forming a glittering wake behind them.

After her initial gasp of shock, Sally tumbled about in the water, surprised at how refreshing it was, the waves' buoyancy lifting her and carrying her from the beach.

She could see Neil's body, a lightness in the dark of the night, as he set off, his powerful crawl pulling him swiftly through the waves.

'Not too far,' she muttered hastily, getting to her feet and watching his every move. But she needn't have worried, for he surfaced again and as quickly returned to her side, sitting beside her as she crouched on the sand.

'I'm not much of a swimmer,' she apologised.

'You should have said.' Quickly he got to his feet, shook back his wet hair and pulled her up to him. 'We can go for a stroll if you'd rather.'

'Much rather.' She glanced back at the sea as they went up the small incline. 'No wonder Hilary wasn't too keen,' Sally muttered as she quickly took Neil's hand. 'There's something almost primeval about that blackness. I'm sure there must be all sorts of strange creatures waiting to pounce.'

'You dopey thing,' Neil teased. 'Nothing will be able to harm you when I'm here to protect you.'

'OK, Tarzan, I'll believe you.'

'Tarzan, perhaps, but I'm not swinging through the trees even for you, my love. This is much more my scene.'

Did I imagine Neil's words just then? Sally wondered, swinging her robe in her free hand as she walked beside him. Did he really call me his 'love'?

'God, those fabulously long legs,' he muttered, staring down admiringly.

His hand was cool, still damp from his swim, and a salty tang filled her nostrils as the moisture evaporated from his body. They ambled in companionable silence, Sally content just to be with him.

'Not too cold?' He turned his head towards her, his face momentarily clear in the moonlight.

'No, it's like paradise.'

'Good. I'm glad to have you to myself. We haven't had any time to really talk lately; life's been too busy.'

Sally sighed, her happiness increasing by the minute.

'What shall we talk about?' she laughed.

'How about you and me?' The answer was so unexpected that she nearly tripped, and would have fallen if Neil's strong grip hadn't steadied her.

'What about us?' she croaked.

'Do you realise, we've never formalised your contract of employment? Every time we tried to get it sorted, someone or something interrupted us.'

Well, you have to reach the peaks to know the troughs, Sally gulped to herself, the crashing disappointment almost unbearable.

'I didn't realise you wanted to discuss work.' She gestured at the velvet night, a fantasy come true. 'How could you think of anything so mundane?'

'Sally, look at me.' Gently Neil pulled her to a halt, and turned her to face him. 'Sally, would you like a more permanent contract?'

'Actually, I've been thinking lately that although I enjoy the job at Kynaston, I should return to more formal nursing soon.'

'Oh, you didn't say.' His voice rose in surprise.

'Well, as you so rightly pointed out, we've had very little time to talk about the future.'

She gazed everywhere but directly at Neil, afraid that her love and longing could be read in her eyes.

'Sally, shall I tell you why I asked you to come on this trip?' He spoke quietly, an almost pleading note in his voice.

'Why?'

'I hated the idea that you might think badly of me.'

'Badly of you? I never. . .'

'Shh, let me finish.' He rested a finger lightly on her mouth. 'You do disapprove of cosmetic surgery, as such—admit it.'

'I don't exactly disapprove. . .'

'You don't like to think of people with money having any advantage in medicine?'

'That's true, but. . .'

'Well, that's why I brought you here, to show you I have another side.'

'And I'm very impressed. But I would still have regarded you highly.'

'Funny,' he said softly. 'I don't usually care what people think of me, but with you. . .' Huskily he whispered her name. 'Sally. . .oh, Sally. . .' Gently he cupped her face in his hands and kissed her.

'I thought we were discussing work,' she said breathlessly as he released her.

'You may be talking about work, but I. . .' He kissed her again, this time pulling her close. She savoured the salty taste of his mouth, breathed in the tang of his still damp skin. Straining against his powerful body, her mouth opened under his, her eyes closed.

'You do feel something for me,' he breathed as she pulled away.

'Is this some sort of test? You don't have to worry that I'll take it too seriously; Trish already warned me that you're wedded to your work.' She was amazed her voice was steady.

'Sally, my love, I've been wanting to take you in my

arms for so long, and. . .I want to ask you a personal question. Who is Tom?'

Sally shifted from one foot to the other. 'Tom is someone from my past. We went out together for a while but now he's working in Texas.'

'What was he doing at the clinic, then?'

'He was home for a couple of weeks' leave.'

'And he means nothing to you now?'

'Nothing at all.'

'That's good,' Neil whispered. He leant forward and kissed her gently on the mouth. 'That's very good.'

'Hey, Neil.' Mike's voice echoing out of the darkness was as shocking as an explosion. 'Neil, where are you? There's an emergency.'

'Damn! Damn and blast.' Turning towards the light that glowed beneath the palm trees, Neil shouted back. 'Coming!'

With smooth strides, he hurried up the slope to where Mike's outline was visible.

'What's the matter?'

'One of the palates we repaired yesterday is bleeding. I don't know how badly; Hilary's gone ahead to have a look.'

'You'd better change, Sally, we may have to do a repair.'

Swiftly he walked ahead with Mike, his questions coming thick and fast, leaving a confused and disturbed Sally bringing up the rear.

By the time she had pulled a cotton tunic over her still damp swimsuit, Neil and Mike were in the theatre. The teenage girl, her thick glossy hair tied back from her face, lay sleeping on the table.

'I think the bleeding-point is just by the soft palate,' Hilary said, quickly packing the mouth with a length of gauze to stop the gush of blood.

'Perhaps one of the ties has slipped.' Neil frowned. 'Let's try pressure on the bleeding-point. If that doesn't work, I'll have to see if I can find the offending artery.'

Sally waited quietly, not giving any indication of her inner turmoil. The brief scene on the beach was hardly believable, and she pinched her arm to make it seem real. What had Neil been about to say? Whatever it was, the opportunity had now gone. He was back to the person she knew better—the dynamic but, she now realised, deeply caring surgeon.

CHAPTER TEN

'I DON'T know about "Washed my hair last night, and can't do a thing with it",' Sally moaned. 'I must have washed my legs as well, for I can't do a thing with them either.'

'For goodness' sake, take your hand away. How can I get your hair to stay in place if you keep undoing all my good work?'

'Sorry, Jane.' Taking a deep breath, Sally stared at her friend's reflection alongside her own and clasped her hands in her lap, trying to still their trembling.

'It's beautiful hair,' Jane mumbled around the clips in her mouth, 'but it's so soft.' Carefully she pulled the brush once more through the thick dark waves, twisting them into a coil at the nape of Sally's neck.

'There, what do you think of that?' Proudly Jane stood back and waited.

'It's lovely.' Amazed, Sally studied herself in the mirror. 'I didn't realise you were so good with hair. It makes my face look almost classical.'

'That's the effect I was hoping to create, like a Greek goddess, to go with the dress.'

They both turned and looked at the shimmer of gold hanging on the outside of the wardrobe. The tissue-fine material fell in soft pleats from neckline to hem, its richness softening the severity of the dress's lines.

'It's really lovely. I'd better finish getting ready, I

suppose.' Shrugging off her bathrobe, Sally took the dress from the hanger and slipped it carefully over her head, clipping the narrow belt into place.

'What do you think?'

'Fabulous!' Jane applauded. 'You look marvellous.'

'I do look pretty good, don't I? I wish you and Matthew were able to be there.'

'Matthew's away, and there's no way I'd want to go on my own.'

'You don't think these splits at the side are a bit much? I'm showing an awful lot of leg.'

'I don't think anything, except that you're to go out there and stun everybody, especially Neil,' Jane said firmly. 'I'm still waiting to hear what happened in Brazil, by the way. I know there's something you haven't told me.' Jane paused, staring hopefully at Sally, who gazed back wide-eyed, not saying a word. 'Oh, well. Perhaps another time. What time is Neil coming to collect you?'

Walking into the sitting-room, Sally looked at the old-fashioned mantel clock. 'Should be here any minute. Thanks Jane. You're a love. I'd never have had the nerve to wear. . . Oh, that's the front door.'

'Stop chewing your lip, you'll have no lipstick left.

Do you want me to answer?'

'Please.'

Briskly Jane called through the entryphone, and Sally stood like a statue as Neil's footsteps gradually mounted the stairs. There was a sharp rap of knuckles and the door to her flat swung open.

'All ready, Sally? Wow!' For a long moment Neil said no more, just stood and gazed at her, his jaw almost dropping. 'Well, Miss Chalmers, you look sensational.'

'Thank you.' Shyly Sally went towards him and took his proffered arm.

'Taxi's waiting, but by rights it should be a coach and horses.'

'I'm not that much of a shock, am I?' She glanced up at him, the broadcloth of his suit smooth under her hand.

Neil didn't answer, just stared at her assessingly.

'Have a good time. I'll lock up here.' Ushering them to the door, Jane gave Sally a knowing wink as she turned to say good-bye, but the impatient shrilling of the telephone stopped them in their tracks.

'Damn. I'd better answer it.' Swiftly Sally went back inside. 'It's the clinic for you.' She passed the receiver to Neil, pretending not to notice Jane's curious frown.

'Sorry about this,' Neil muttered. 'I won't be a moment.'

'Wonder what the problem is?' Sally said softly to Jane.

'He did what? What excuse did he offer. . .?'

Both Jane and Sally gaped at the anger in Neil's voice. 'I'll be there in ten minutes. Don't let him get away.'

'Sorry to mess up our plans, but I have to get back to Kynaston.'

'What's the matter?' Anxiously Sally rested a hand on his arm.

'It's Melody.'

To her bewilderment, he looked furious rather than upset, his grey eyes glinting, his mouth drawn into a thin line that altered the whole shape of his lower face.

'Is she ill?' Heart beating fast, Sally stared up at him.

'No, an unwelcome visitor.'

'Can't the night staff—who's on? Kathy?—Can't she ask him or her to go? Who is the visitor?'

'Some wretched reporter. . .I'll have to see to it myself.' Angrily Neil ran a finger round the inside of his collar.

'I'll come with you.'

'There's really no need. I'll sort it out and pick you up later.'

'Please, I'd like to come. I've become very fond of Melody and I know I can help.'

'Well, if you're sure. We can get there very quickly, if we're lucky with the traffic.'

Taking her hand, he towed Sally down the stairs.

'Not so fast,' Sally protested, holding the hem of her skirt in her free hand. But he didn't hear her, just hurried her through the main front door.

The taxi's engine was already revving as he pushed Sally into the rear seat and clambered in after her.

'Did you say something about a reporter?' Pulling her skirt free from under her, Sally shifted herself into a more comfortable position. So much for coach and horses and being treated like Dresden china, she thought ruefully.

'Kathy thought he was a friend from the studio and let him in, stupid girl. Wait till I see her. She went back after a few minutes with some coffee and discovered him with a camera. She still didn't think anything of it until Melody complained.'

'But won't he be gone by the time we get there?'

'Well, he'd refused to leave when Kathy rang, so with a bit of luck, he'll still be there.'

'But does it matter that much? After all, Melody had her splints removed when we got back the day before yesterday.' Sally was puzzled by the seething rage she could sense coming from Neil. Even his skin gave off a sharp aroma, a smell closely akin to fear. And his arm, when she accidentally brushed against it as the taxi rounded a sharp bend, was as tight as a tourniquet.

'I know Melody has had her splints off,' he said, 'but I don't want her poor bruised face all over the papers. Nor does her family.'

'I wonder how he managed to discover. . .? Oh, sorry.' Once again Sally was propelled across the seat, almost on to Neil's lap.

'That's all right.' Neil barely acknowledged her struggle to sit upright. 'Someone must have mentioned Melody to a friend, or in a pub, possibly. It's almost impossible to keep something like this a complete secret. In fact, I'm surprised, in a way, that we haven't had trouble before.'

Not Tom, Sally prayed silently, remembering his interest. He wouldn't, surely?

Shortly after, they turned into the drive of the clinic, and Neil leapt from the vehicle almost before it stopped, racing up the three steps to the front door.

'Wait for me,' Sally muttered, hurrying after Neil. 'What about paying?' she called.

'I'll send a bill. Mr Lawrence has an account with our firm,' the taxi driver told her. 'Don't you worry about it.'

'I'm not worried about the bill,' Sally exclaimed as she raced along the corridor. 'But the state Neil is in, he's likely to thump anyone that gets in his way.'

She heard the voices before reaching Melody's room—a protesting shout from one, interrupted by Neil's deep smooth tones, still recognisable despite his anger.

Quickly she pushed back the door, and saw a small man in leather jacket and jeans standing with his back to the window. Neil, his expression cold, loomed menacingly.

'If you lay a finger on my cameras,' the visitor blustered, 'I'll sue you for everything. . .'

'Go ahead, sue me. But I want that film.'

'Melody, are you all right?' Sally flung her bag on the edge of the bed and put her arm around the patient's shoulder. Nervously Melody nodded as she took Sally's comforting hand.

Sally still couldn't understand Neil's anger. She had seen him furious before—witness when Melody had been so upset by the sight of her face—but, even so, Neil's reaction in the present situation did seem extreme.

Smiling at Melody, Sally crossed the room to Neil's side. 'Don't you think it might be better to continue your discussion outside?' Resting a hand on his arm, she tried to steer him gently away.

'Let me alone, Sally. This isn't your affair.' Impatiently he shook his arm free. 'Now, are you going to give me that film or. . .?'

'Or what?' the other man sneered.

'Or do I report you to. . .?'

'Oh, what's the point in arguing? I can always come back with a telescopic lens.' Opening the back of his camera, he threw the film on to the bed.

'Now, get out.'

'Glad to. Wasn't much of a story, anyway. Except that she's probably finished in television. I suppose a few people might be interested to know that.'

'Neil!' Hastily Sally seized his arm once more. 'That's not the way to deal with it.'

'I could kill him.' Hands shaking, Neil sank back on to the bedside chair as the visitor hurried through the door.

'That wouldn't be very good publicity, now would it?' Sally said quietly.

Taking a deep breath, Neil ran his fingers through his hair. 'Are you all right, Melody?'

'Yes, thanks. I had no idea he was a reporter, thought he was a friend of Paul's.' She giggled.

'What's so funny?'

'It was his face when Neil burst into the room— absolute horror—then when you came in, Sally, he couldn't take his eyes off you.' Melody giggled again. 'Gaping with desire.'

'Just as well I didn't see that,' Neil said fiercely. 'I certainly wouldn't have been able to keep my hands off him.'

'You don't mean that, Neil. Violence never solved anything. And think what damage you could have done to your hands if. . .' Sally broke off, aware of the speculative light in Neil's eyes, a light that made her catch her breath. She looked away.

'Melody, are you sure you're feeling OK?'

'Quite sure.' The young girl shrugged. 'I was think-ing, What does it matter if my face is shown as it is now?' She brushed her upper jaw with her fingertips. 'When I've recovered completely, it'll just prove what a marvellous job Neil has made of the repair.'

'Melody, you shame me. Such a mature attitude, the most grown-up in the room,' Neil sighed.

Raising her eyebrows at Neil's remark—after all, *she* hadn't lost her temper—Sally went to the door. 'How about coffee, you two?'

'Sally,' Melody called after her.

'Yes?'

'You look fabulous.' There was no envy in Melody's voice, just wholehearted admiration.

'Thanks, Melody,'

'She does look good, doesn't she?' Sitting upright in the chair, Neil leaned forward and took Melody's hand.

'Don't take any notice of that ignorant so-and-so, or his remarks about your working. Your looks are important, I agree, but personality is vital as well, and yours really shines. And your courage.'

'I've had time to think while I've been here, and when I look back I was lucky to get away with only facial injuries, wasn't I? I could have fractured my skull or my spine, been much more severely injured.'

'Quite the little philosopher.' Neil grinned. There was a knock at the door.

'I thought you might like coffee.' Kathy appeared with a tray. 'I'm terribly sorry about letting that man in.' Her chubby face was shiny with embarrassment.

'Don't worry. We all make mistakes, and as it hap-pened there was no real harm done.' Neil took the tray and set it on the bedside table. 'Thank you, Kathy. Right,' he said firmly. 'Let's have our drink and then we can get to the ball.' He picked up the jug and poured the coffee, sniffing appreciatively.

'Actually, I'd be quite happy to give it a miss. Thank you.' Sally took her cup from Neil's outstretched hand.

'What? But I thought you were looking forward to it.'

'Well, yes, I was, I suppose,' Sally said slowly, not sure if it was true or not. At least this was they would avoid Fiona. 'But I'd just as soon stay and chat to Melody for a while. Would you mind, Neil? You go, if you want to. I don't mind.' Quickly she crossed her fingers at the blatant fib.

'Well, thanks, that's really flattering,' Neil frowned. 'Here's your coffee, Melody, milky to make it cool.' He went back to his chair and picked up his own cup. 'Actually, it's probably getting pretty rowdy there by now.'

'Don't spoil your evening because of me.' Melody looked worried.

'We want to stay,' Sally repeated. 'What shall we do? Would you fancy a game of Scrabble?'

'Well, if you're sure.' Quickly Melody drained her cup.

'I should warn you, Neil, Melody is very good.' Sally set out the board and collected paper and pencil. 'But this time I'm determined to win.'

Not what I expected from my romantic night out, she thought, remembering the search for the perfect dress, the brand new make-up, Jane's help with her hair.

Her fantasy picture of herself and Neil on the dance-floor had shown Neil holding her close, his hand at her waist, his face pressed lightly against her own, his own special aroma in her nostrils—it all couldn't be further from the truth.

She had imagined a stroll in grounds scented with nicotiana and stock, an occasional chirrup from a sleepy bird the only sound to disturb their closeness. Perhaps a chance to continue the unfinished business on the beach. . .

Grinning ruefully at the difference between dreams and reality, Sally glanced up from her Scrabble letters to find Neil studying her intently. He'd removed his bow tie, and the crisp, unrelieved white-ness of his shirt emphasised his tan more strongly than ever.

'Penny for them,' he murmured.

'Nothing worth a penny.'

He shrugged and looked back at the board, but there was something in the depths of those grey eyes that reminded her of how he had gazed at her on Setuba. And her heart beat faster.

In a way, it was surprising that Neil hadn't said anything since their return. But the clinic had been busy, a backlog of cases waiting—two face-lifts, a removal of scarring from an old tattoo, a breast reduction, and a reshaping of a jaw, that had brought Melody's surgery vividly to mind.

Sally had tried to reassure herself that being busy was the reason Neil hadn't followed up the conversation he had started; she couldn't bear the alternative—that he might have regrets, that the balmy tropical night and moonlight had led him to say more than he had intended.

Suddenly she noticed the silence, and realized that Melody and Neil were staring curiously at her.

'You start, Melody,' she ordered quickly.

'Right. How about this? F.A.C.I.A.L. Double word score gives me twenty two.'

'How appropriate,' laughed Sally as she followed with her own letters. The game continued in silence, apart from an occasional comment and answer from Melody and Sally. Neil seemed abstracted and barely concentrating; as the game progressed it was apparent that he would be easily beaten.

'I don't think you spell "musth" like that, Melody,' Sally laughed as the game gradually drew to a close.

'You can do. It means a male elephant in a state of sexual excitement,' Melody said innocently.

'Are you sure you're not making it up? What do you think, Neil, should we allow it?'

'If Melody says it's right, I'm sure it is.'

'God, what a thought,' Sally muttered as she quickly wrote down the scores. 'An elephant in a state of sexual excitement! Melody,' she added, 'you've won again.'

'Well, it's probably not really fair,' Melody apologised. 'We play a lot between takes when we're filming and, in fact, I was one of the best.'

'Didn't think you had any free time at all. Thought it was an eighteen-hour day, filming one scene, rehearsing another.'

'It can be like that, Sally. Normally they aim to get one and a half minutes' viewable film completed every day, but sometimes soaps are more concentrated.'

Melody settled back more comfortably against the pillows, her ankles crossed in front of her. 'But even then there are gaps when you need to find something else to do.' She yawned suddenly. 'Oh, you can't believe how good it is to get rid of all that ironwork, to be able to open my mouth properly.'

'I expect your face feels a bit insecure at the moment, doesn't it?' It had been so long since Neil had spoken that both Sally and Melody jumped. He had so obviously been lost in thoughts that at times put a heavy frown on his face that Sally had decided it was perhaps better not to try to drag him into the conversation.

'It does a bit,' Melody said thoughtfully. 'But just think, at long last I'll be able to eat something normal.'

'Hamburger?' Neil grinned

'Mmm, yummy, and pizza and chips with curry sauce.'

'That's what I call a really healthy diet,' he laughed. 'Now you'd better get some sleep. I'll see you in the morning.' He leaned across the bed and tapped her lightly on the nose, then escorted Sally from the room. 'Having completely spoilt your evening, what would you like to do?' They moved slowly towards his office door. 'It's only ten o'clock; we could go to the ball, if you like. We've missed dinner, but there'll still be plenty going on. Or. . .' He paused.

'Or what?' Sally said softly.

'We could have a quiet drink together. I've got some good malt whisky in my room. Or a brandy.'

'A whisky sounds a good idea.'

Leading the way, Neil switched on the lamp over the desk and went to a cupboard in the corner.

The amber fluid in cut-glass tumblers split the light into a rainbow spray of colour as Sally thoughtfully twirled her glass. With a sigh, she sank back in an armchair and kicked off her shoes.

'You will have to let me make up to you for this evening.' Neil sat opposite her, leaning forward, his elbows resting on his knees.

'Don't be silly, there's nothing to make up for. It was a most memorable evening, and I wouldn't have missed the excitement for the world.' She sipped her drink. 'Though you're pretty scary when you're annoyed, aren't you?' She giggled suddenly. 'I wonder what that reporter thought when he first saw you?'

'I tell you what, if I'd noticed him lusting after you, I definitely wouldn't have been able to keep my hands off him.' He shook his head. 'You're a love. I invite you to go with me to the ball in a pretty tactless fashion, suggesting that it's to protect me from Fiona, then your evening—for which you look absolutely stunning——' he saluted her with his glass '—ends up here at work, in what could have been very unpleasant circumstances, and you sit quite happily sipping Scotch and accepting the whole situation with perfect calm.'

'Whoa, I don't think I can take all these compliments in one go.' Thank God for dim lighting, she thought, her face aglow.

'And my only excuse is that nothing has turned out as I planned. If it weren't for your nice nature. . .'

'Yuk,' Sally interrupted.

'But it's true.' He got up from his chair and crouched beside hers. 'And your ability to remain calm; that's why I knew you'd be right to meet and greet the clients.' He took her hand and gently smoothed the back with his thumb. 'Can I ask you something personal?'

'Again? We seem to have trodden this road before.' Calm? She'd never felt less calm in her life. 'Just how personal?'

Ignoring her question, Neil took the glass from her nerveless fingers, set it on the desk, and pulled her to her feet. 'That lovely skin,' he murmured throatily, trailing his lips down her cheek to the corner of her mouth.

'Neil,' Sally protested. 'What are you doing?'

'Isn't it obvious?' He laughed softly. 'You have no idea how much I've longed to continue what we started in Setuba.'

Her uncertainties were gone, melted in the warmth of his mouth on hers. All her doubts dissolved as she was stirred into a response that betrayed how much she had been yearning for this moment.

And, to her soaring delight, it seemed as though Neil felt the same. Mouth on mouth, thigh against thigh, they strained together, their breath intermingled.

Sally's hair, so carefully set by Jane, tumbled about her head as Neil's questing hands ran through it, questing hands that gradually slid down the length of her spine and inside the openings at the side of her dress. His fingers softly stroked the bare skin at her waist, and moved towards the soft swell of her breasts, the burning of his kiss a sweet torment that drove all sense from her brain.

She was completely lost, and it was Neil who heard

the slamming of a door in the distance and released her so suddenly that she staggered on to the chair behind her.

Trembling, Sally pushed aside the dark tresses that had fallen over her face.

'Sorry.' Neil took a deep, shuddering breath. 'Like the elephant, I must have had an attack of "musth".' His quiet laugh was strained as he turned to face her. 'No, I'm not going to apologise, for I'm *not* sorry. Only if I've upset you.'

'Of course you haven't upset me.' Quickly Sally got to her feet and moved towards him. Delicately she touched his face. 'It's just that I'm not sure. . .'

'Haven't I made it obvious?' He turned his face towards her exploring hand and pressed a kiss on the palm.

'It's been such an oddball night, I didn't want your lovemaking to be for the wrong reasons,' she murmured.

'And what would you call the right reasons?' he asked drily, his grey eyes searching her face.

'I don't know.' She shrugged, her heartbeat so strong it almost choked her.

'Sally, can I ask you a personal question?'

'You keep saying that and, as I said before, personal questions make me nervous.'

'You'd better prepare to be really nervous, then,' he said softly. 'For this is as personal as you can get.' He paused. 'Will you marry me? Is that personal enough?'

'Are you serious?' she gulped.

'Never been more serious in my life.' He brushed

her hair back from her face. 'Come on, it can't be that much of a shock, you must have guessed. . .'

'I had no idea.' She waved her hands in disbelief. 'I knew you found me attractive, knew you appreciated my work. . .' She stopped, unable to say any more for the pounding in her ears.

'You're sexy, I like your even temperament, I can't resist your lovely legs, or the softness of your skin. . .'

He still hadn't said it, she thought, scarcely able to breathe as she waited.

'And?' she prompted.

'Isn't that enough?' She could sense his bewilderment.

'No, it's not.' She moved to the window, watching his reflection in the darkened glass as he studied her.

'What else is there?' He moved across the room and stood behind her. 'I thought you cared for me. Don't you love me?'

'Aha, there's the magic word. You haven't said. . .'

He pulled her close. 'Oh, you. . .' He nuzzled at her neck. 'You had me worried. I love you, I love you, I love you, I love you. I want you to be my wife.' Every remark was punctuated with tiny kisses.

'And I love you, too, Neil,' she murmured, turning to face him.

'So you will consider a permanent position, then? As my wife?'

'Yes, please.'

'I can't believe you had no idea how I felt about you.' He smoothed her hair back from her uptilted face. 'So much to talk about, so much to discuss,' he murmured softly, nibbling the lobe of her ear, trailing kisses over her face and neck, sending small ripples of sensation through her. Abruptly he stopped.

'Come on, let's finish our drink, then I must take you home, or I might end up like the elephant, unable to control my "musth".'

'Must we?'

'God, what a terrible pun,' Neil groaned. 'Yes, we must.'

And their laughter echoed in the room as they picked up their glasses and raised them in a salute that held so much promise—a promise of a future together.

MILLS & BOON

JANUARY 1995 HARDBACK TITLES

Romance

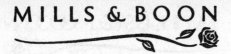

MILLS & BOON

JANUARY 1995 LARGE PRINT TITLES

Romance

The Sun at Midnight *Sandra Field*	775	0 263 14036 9
More Than Lovers *Natalie Fox*	776	0 263 14037 7
Leonie's Luck *Emma Goldrick*	777	0 263 14038 5
Angel of Darkness *Lynne Graham*	778	0 263 14039 3
Brittle Bondage *Anne Mather*	779	0 263 14040 7
Wild Injustice *Margaret Mayo*	780	0 263 14041 5
Duel in the Sun *Sally Wentworth*	781	0 263 14042 3
Sense of Destiny *Patricia Wilson*	782	0 263 14043 1

LEGACY*of*LOVE

Conqueror's Lady *Gail Mallin*	0 263 14181 0
Reasons of the Heart *Paula Marshall*	0 263 14182 9

LOVE ON CALL

Midnight Sun *Rebecca Lang*	0 263 14169 1
One Caring Heart *Marion Lennox*	0 263 14170 5

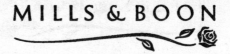

MILLS & BOON

FEBRUARY 1995 HARDBACK TITLES

Romance

Forever Isn't Long Enough *Val Daniels*	H4212	0 263 14243 4
The Shining of Love *Emma Darcy*	H4213	0 263 14244 2
Unwelcome Invader *Angela Devine*	H4214	0 263 14245 0
Untouched *Sandra Field*	H4215	0 263 14246 9
Thief of Hearts *Natalie Fox*	H4216	0 263 14247 7
A Brief Encounter *Catherine George*	H4217	0 263 14248 5
Secret Obsession *Charlotte Lamb*	H4218	0 263 14249 3
A Very Secret Affair *Miranda Lee*	H4219	0 263 14250 7
Triumph of Love *Barbara McMahon*	H4220	0 263 14251 5
A Circle of Opals *Wynne May*	H4221	0 263 14252 3
Dearest Love *Betty Neels*	H4222	0 263 14253 1
Jungle Fever *Jennifer Taylor*	H4223	0 263 14254 X
Fire and Spice *Karen van der Zee*	H4224	0 263 14255 8
The Wedding Effect *Sophie Weston*	H4225	0 263 14256 6
Beyond All Reason *Cathy Williams*	H4226	0 263 14257 4
Free to Love *Alison York*	H4227	0 263 14258 2

LEGACY *of* LOVE

The Last Enchantment *Meg Alexander*	M353	0 263 14323 6
Marriage Rites *Pauline Bentley*	M354	0 263 14324 4

LOVE ON CALL

Crisis Point *Grace Read*	D271	0 263 14327 9
A Subtle Magic *Meredith Webber*	D272	0 263 14328 7

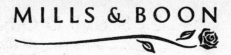

MILLS & BOON

FEBRUARY 1995 LARGE PRINT TITLES

Romance

A Masterful Man *Lindsay Armstrong*	783	0 263 14071 7
Web of Darkness *Helen Brooks*	784	0 263 14072 5
Dark Apollo *Sara Craven*	785	0 263 14073 3
Waiting Game *Diana Hamilton*	786	0 263 14074 1
Dark Fate *Charlotte Lamb*	787	0 263 14075 X
Dearest Mary Jane *Betty Neels*	788	0 263 14076 8
A Wayward Love *Emma Richmond*	789	0 263 14077 6
Tangled Destinies *Sara Wood*	790	0 263 14078 4

LEGACY of LOVE

House of Secrets *Sally Blake*	0 263 14183 7
Eleanor *Sylvia Andrew*	0 263 14184 5

LOVE ON CALL

Role Play *Caroline Anderson*	0 263 14171 3
Conflicting Loyalties *Lilian Darcy*	0 263 14172 1